GH00854250

The Zombie

Books 1 to 6

Mark Mulle

PUBLISHED BY:

Mark Mulle

TABLE OF CONTENTS

A ZOMBIE SUMMER SCHOOL DIARY
BOOK 1: MY TEACHER IS A SKELETON
....21

DAY ONE: INTRODUCING MYSELF 21

DAY TWO: THE FIRST DAY OF SUMMER
SCHOOL 24

DAY THREE: NO WAY 27

DAY FOUR: MY PLAN 29

DAY FIVE: THE FIRST ASSIGNMENT ...31

DAY SIX: PRESENTATION DAY 34

DAY SEVEN: LIFE AT HOME 37

DAY EIGHT: MY PAL, GRUNT 40

DAY NINE: A NEW LESSON 43

DAY TEN: MY HISTORY TEACHER WAS A SOLDIER? 46

DAY ELEVEN: RESEARCH DAY 49

DAY TWELVE: ANOTHER ASSIGNMENT 52

DAY THIRTEEN: WHAT WOULD I DO?54

DAY FOURTEEN: NERD? 56

DAY FIFTEEN: A SECOND OPINION ...59

DAY SIXTEEN: INSPIRED BY A DREAM 62

DAY SEVENTEEN: YOU'RE ONLY IN TROUBLE IF YOU GET CAUGHT 65

DAY EIGHTEEN: AN UPRISING IN THE KINGDOM OF COOL 68

DAY NINETEEN: ROLE REVERSAL......70

DAY TWENTY: LOOK, BUT DON'T TOUCH 73

DAY TWENTY-ONE: MY NEW FRIEND, SNOW 76

DAY TWENTY-TWO: MORE ABOUT SKELETONS 79

DAY TWENTY-THREE: ZOMBIE LESSON 82

DAY TWENTY-FOUR: THE MANY ADVENTURES OF MS. SKELE 85

DAY TWENTY-FIVE: THE LAST ASSIGNMENT..88

DAY TWENTY-SIX: THE DARK AGES 91

DAY TWENTY-SEVEN: THE LAST DAY OF HISTORY CLASS 94

DAY TWENTY-EIGHT: GRUNT'S GRUNTING...96

DAY TWENTY-NINE: NEXT ON THE SCHEDULE... 99

DAY THIRTY: THE LETTER 102

BOOK 2: MY SCIENCE TEACHER IS A WITCH................................104

DAY ONE: MY HISTORY TEACHER WAS A SKELETON 104

DAY TWO: THE FIRST DAY OF SCIENCE CLASS.............................107

DAY THREE: SOMETHING CALLED A SYLLABUS 110

DAY FOUR: LAB SAFETY 113

DAY FIVE: THE FIRST REAL LAB.........116

DAY SIX: TESTING THE EXPERIMENTS 119

DAY SEVEN: GRUNT'S HOUSE.............122

DAY EIGHT: A CALL HOME 125

DAY NINE: TUTORING 129

DAY TEN: TALKING AND TROUBLE ..132

DAY ELEVEN: ANOTHER LAB, ANOTHER MISTAKE..............................135

DAY TWELVE: DETENTION 138

DAY THIRTEEN: BETTER AND WORSE 141

DAY FOURTEEN: SNOW'S HOUSE 144

DAY FIFTEEN: ROARBERT'S BROTHERLY TALKS 146

DAY SIXTEEN: MORE ABOUT MISS ENCHANTMENT.....................................149

DAY SEVENTEEN: ALL ABOUT WITCHES..152

DAY EIGHTEEN: ANOTHER LAB DAY 154

DAY NINETEEN: THE RESULTS 157

DAY TWENTY: TRYING TO TALK........160

DAY TWENTY-ONE: SNOW AND HER CREW..............................163

DAY TWENTY-TWO: AM I A WIZARD? 166

DAY TWENTY-THREE: WHO CAN BE MAGIC?.......................................169

DAY TWENTY-FOUR: BAD NEWS AND WORRIES 172

DAY TWENTY-FIVE: SCHEDULING A STUDY SESSION 175

DAY TWENTY-SIX: FRENEMIES NO MORE 178

DAY TWENTY-SEVEN: TEST DAY........181

DAY TWENTY-EIGHT: THE BEST OF FRIENDS.....................................183

DAY TWENTY-NINE: PASSING PARTY 186

DAY THIRTY: WHAT'S NEXT? 189

BOOK 3: MY GYM TEACHER IS A BLAZE 191

DAY ONE: PASSING CLASSES 191

DAY TWO: FRIENDS IN DIFFERENT PLACES 194

DAY THREE: THE FIRST DAY OF GYM 197

DAY FOUR: THE CHALLENGE 200

DAY FIVE: DODGEBALL 203

DAY SIX: PICKED LAST 206

DAY SEVEN: KIDS LIKE ME 208

DAY EIGHT: SNOW AND GRUNT 211

DAY NINE: ROARBERT'S SECRET 214

DAY TEN: LOST AND ON A RUN 217

DAY ELEVEN: HIGH PRAISE 220

9

DAY TWELVE: BASEBALL......................223

DAY THIRTEEN: FENCING, AKA
SWORD FIGHTING..................................226

DAY FOURTEEN: FRIDAY FREE DAY 228

DAY FIFTEEN: FENCING WITH
ROARBERT AND GRUNT 230

DAY SIXTEEN: SNOW'S SURPRISE 233

DAY SEVENTEEN: TESTS? AGAIN?.....236

DAY EIGHTEEN: VOLLEYBALL 239

DAY NINETEEN: CONFUSED, BUT
HAPPY...242

DAY TWENTY: SKY..................................244

DAY TWENTY-ONE: BEACH FREE DAY
....247

DAY TWENTY-TWO: THE FRIENDS OF
MY FRIENDS ARE MY FRIENDS..........250

DAY TWENTY-THREE: WHAT TIME IS IT? BRO TIME. 253

DAY TWENTY-FOUR: THE BEGINNING OF CHALLENGE WEEK 256

DAY TWENTY-FIVE: DODGEBALL CHALLENGE 259

DAY TWENTY-SIX: VOLLEYBALL CHALLENGE 262

DAY TWENTY-SEVEN: BASEBALL CHALLENGE 265

DAY TWENTY-EIGHT: FENCING CHALLENGE 268

DAY TWENTY-NINE: PARTY TIME!....271

DAY THIRTY: PACKING UP..........274

THE ZOMBIE MIDDLE SCHOOL DIARY BOOK 4: MY HOME ECONOMICS TEACHER IS A PIGMAN 276

DAY ONE: THE LAST DAY OF SUMMER VACATION 276

DAY TWO: THE FIRST DAY OF MIDDLE SCHOOL 280

DAY THREE: INTRODUCING...............283

DAY FOUR: HOME EC? MORE LIKE HILARIOUS EC..286

DAY FIVE: SNOW AND TIBBY'S ADVENTURES 289

DAY SIX: THE ASSEMBLY......................292

DAY SEVEN: TALKING WITH ROARBERT 295

DAY EIGHT: ZOMBIE MEETS OVERWORLD 299

DAY NINE: SEWING 302

DAY TEN: A MEAL WITH THE GIRLS.305

DAY ELEVEN: SIGNING UP 309

DAY TWELVE: A SEWING SITUATION311

DAY THIRTEEN: BEHAVING BETTER
....314

DAY FOURTEEN: HAPPY BIRTHDAY TO ME!...316

DAY FIFTEEN: TIME TO CHILL 319

DAY SIXTEEN: THE COOKING CLUB.321

DAY SEVENTEEN: OTHER CLUBS 323

DAY EIGHTEEN: CLUB MEETS CLASSROOM 325

DAY NINETEEN: KITCHEN TUTOR ..327

DAY TWENTY: THE BAKE SALE BAKE OFF 330

DAY TWENTY-ONE: BOYS ONLY!.......333

DAY TWENTY-TWO: A DAY OUT WITH THE GIRLS...335

DAY TWENTY-THREE: THE COOKING CLUB, AGAIN...339

DAY TWENTY-FOUR: GRUNT'S GRUNTS
....342

DAY TWENTY-FIVE: ROARBERT'S
BROTHERLY ADVICE 344

DAY TWENTY-SIX: FINALLY TALKING
....347

DAY TWENTY-SEVEN: SUMMER
MEMORIES AND AUTUMN IDEAS 351

DAY TWENTY-EIGHT: FENCING........353

DAY TWENTY-NINE: PARTY! 356

DAY THIRTY: WHAT NEXT?.................358

BOOK 5: MY ENGLISH SUBSTITUTE
TEACHER...360

DAY ONE: LAST SUMMER 360

DAY TWO: THE FIRST MONTH OF
MIDDLE SCHOOL 364

DAY THREE: A NEW SUBSTITUTE 367

DAY FOUR: ENGLISH CLASS 370

DAY FIVE: THE WEEKEND...................373

DAY SIX: CHILLING WITH MY BRO....376

DAY SEVEN: COOKING CLUB 379

DAY EIGHT: CRIME AND
PUNISHMENT 382

DAY NINE: D IS FOR DIPLOMA 385

DAY TEN: A WEIRD FAVOR 388

DAY ELEVEN: THE PERFECT DATE ..391

DAY TWELVE: THE DOUBLE DATE ...394

DAY THIRTEEN: GIRL TROUBLES 398

DAY FOURTEEN: NOTHING BUT
COOKING 401

DAY FIFTEEN: HALLOWEEN IN THE
HALLS 404

DAY SIXTEEN: "EGGING" ON THE
TEACHER....................................406

DAY SEVENTEEN: EVERYTHING BUT
STUDYING 409

DAY EIGHTEEN: THE TEST AND
ANOTHER FAVOR.....................412

DAY NINETEEN: SOME FRIENDS... ...415

DAY TWENTY: DISGUISING MY
APPEARANCE AND FEELINGS 418

DAY TWENTY-ONE: BURNING UP
INSIDE AND IN THE OVEN.................421

DAY TWENTY-TWO: YA GOTTA DO
WHAT YA GOTTA DO 424

DAY TWENTY-THREE: TAKING THE
EASY WAY OUT 427

DAY TWENTY-FOUR: NONSENSE 429

DAY TWENTY-FIVE: AMBUSH 432

DAY TWENTY-SIX: THE PLAY: ACT ONE 436

DAY TWENTY-SEVEN: THE PLAY: ACT TWO...439

DAY TWENTY-EIGHT: HALLOWEEN TREATS..442

DAY TWENTY-NINE: HALLOWEEN PARTY! 445

DAY THIRTY: NEXT MONTH...............448

BOOK 6: MY WOODSHOP TEACHER IS AN ENDERMAN 450

DAY ONE: MIDDLE SCHOOL 450

DAY TWO: NORMAL AGAIN...................454

DAY THREE: AT THE MALL WITH MY FRIENDS 456

DAY FOUR: LAZY DAY WITH ROARBERT 459

DAY FIVE: THE WOODSHOP PRESENTATION 461

DAY SIX: SHOULD I JOIN? 464

DAY SEVEN: GYM CLASS STINKS LIKE GYM SOCKS 467

DAY EIGHT: MAKING UP MY MIND ...470

DAY NINE: SIGNING UP 473

DAY TEN: THE DOUBLE DATE 475

DAY ELEVEN: CHILLING WITH THE GUYS, LITERALLY 478

DAY TWELVE: WOODSHOP CLASS 481

DAY THIRTEEN: IN THE FOREST......484

DAY FOURTEEN: SAFETY DAY............487

DAY FIFTEEN: PICTURE FRAME DAY 490

DAY SIXTEEN: GYM AGAIN 493

DAY SEVENTEEN: FOLLOWING
ROARBERT'S ADVICE 495

DAY EIGHTEEN: THE DATE...............498

DAY NINETEEN: THE COOKING CLUB
....501

DAY TWENTY: THIS IS LAME: A
MEMOIR OF WOODSHOP CLASS.........504

DAY TWENTY-ONE: BIRDHOUSES.....506

DAY TWENTY-TWO: PAINTING 509

DAY TWENTY-THREE: THE LAST DAY
OF WOODSHOP CLASS 512

DAY TWENTY-FOUR: THINKING...TOO
MUCH...515

DAY TWENTY-FIVE: SNOW'S VISIT.....517

DAY TWENTY-SIX: GOOD NEWS 520

DAY TWENTY-SEVEN: OFFICIAL
EVALUATION..523

DAY TWENTY-EIGHT: RESULTS OF
THE EVALUATION 526

DAY TWENTY-NINE: STUDENT-
PARENT-TEACHER CONFERENCES .529

DAY THIRTY: A BUSY LIFE AND A FULL
DIARY 533

A Zombie Summer School Diary
Book 1: My Teacher is a Skeleton

Day One: Introducing Myself

Dear Diary,

My name is Ugh, and I'm just about the coolest zombie that anyone could ever imagine meeting. I'm truly one of a kind. I'm about to start a new chapter of my life, and it's one that I'm really not excited about. I've just finished the fifth grade...kinda. I kind of have to spend my whole summer in summer school if I want to be able to go into middle school with the rest of my class. I don't have to go to summer school because I'm slow learner or anything like that. I can easily do all of the homework that the teachers hand out; it's just that I don't do the homework that they hand out. Homework just seems like a waste of time to me. There are so many other better things that I could be spending my time on, but the teachers don't seem to agree with me on that issue. Teachers think that homework and tests are the coolest things out there, and if you don't follow their rules then you get left behind.

I got left behind because I managed to fail three classes this year. It's really lucky that I didn't fail four classes or else I would have gotten held back for sure. The thing is, my school's summer program is weird. Each subject is taught for a month, and then the school moves onto the next subject. Since there are only three months of summer, it's a pretty good thing that I only failed three classes. Well, it's bad that I failed any classes, but when it comes to failing, this still isn't a worst-case scenario. The three classes that I need to redo this summer are history, science, and gym. And no, I didn't fail gym just because zombies are slow. I failed gym because I never showed up. I just want to make that clear now.

Anyway, summer school starts tomorrow on Monday night. I would go to school during the day, but the whole being a zombie and burning in the sun prevents that. My mom is also making me write in this diary until summer school is over as a punishment for failing so many classes. I'm going to try to have some fun with it, though. I mean, if I have to write in it, then I might as well write something cool.

Day Two: The First Day of Summer School

Dear Diary,

Today is Monday, and it's the first day of summer school. The class is only about an hour long, so it's not really a whole day, more like a wholly disappointing activity. Anyway, the first class that I need to be a part of is the history class. I bet that it'll be super boring. I'll have to remember to take a nap before class so that I don't fall asleep during it. I mean, that is why I failed this class last time.

When I walked into the classroom I noticed that it wasn't the normal history teacher that was in the classroom. My normal teacher is Mr. Pork. He's an insanely fat Pigman who drones on about only the most boring thing that he can think of for that day. The new teacher was super skinny. When he turned around I realized why: she was a skeleton. I had never had a skeleton teacher before. I mean, most of my teachers had been monsters since I was technically a monster, but most of them at least had eyes. This was a little spooky. Oh, by the way, her name is Ms. Skele.

Luckily, things didn't stay spooky for long because it turned out that one of my friends was in this class too. My friend Grunt was also in my class, failed this class, and was a zombie just like me. To be fair, it was probably my fault that Grunt was in summer school at all. Most of the time when I was skipping class during the school year he was right there next to me.

The rest of the kids in the class weren't there for skipping class, they just weren't the brightest kids on the block. I don't think that I'll be talking to many of them, but it doesn't really matter since I have Grunt to talk to.

Today the teacher just handed out a schedule for what we would be doing for the next couple of weeks. I guess that we would be learning a lot about the Skeleton War this month. I didn't have to think very hard to guess why we would need to do that...

Anyway, I'll be back to this old school tomorrow to learn something or to sleep during class. I guess I just need to wait and see how great this teacher is. I'll write more tomorrow.

Day Three: No Way

Dear Diary,

School was pretty boring today. There wasn't really much to talk about. The teacher kept talking about how cool skeletons are and how they invented some really neat stuff and blah, blah, blah. I really didn't pay much attention to what the teacher was talking about. All my notes say is, "Skeletons are pretty cool, lol." Next to my super descriptive notes is a doodle of some Skeletons shooting arrows at each other. There's no way that I would ever fail an art class with these sweet skills.

One thing in the class did catch my attention, though. One of the kids in their class, I think her name is Izzie, asked our teacher how she knew so much about this stuff. Our teacher kind of shrugged it off and casually told her that she knew all about it because she was there. At first, I let it slide, but then I did some math. If my teacher was there when the Skeleton Wars were a big problem, then that would mean that she's hundreds of years old. There's no way it could be true! Or could it?

I talked to Grunt about my suspicions after class. I asked him if he thought the teacher was serious or not. All he replied was, "I don't know. Why don't you ask her?" This answer really didn't help me at all, mostly because I'm not going to talk to the teacher about it. I don't really like teachers, so I'm not going to talk to them if I don't have to.

I guess I'll just keep waiting for my teacher to drop more hints about her age. It looks like this class is finally going to have something interesting in store for me.

Day Five: The First Assignment

Dear Diary,

I was going to start paying attention today, but Ms. Skele didn't want to talk about her past. She wanted all of us to talk about our pasts. Well, not about our pasts exactly, she wanted us to make family trees. She wanted us to go back as far as we could. The rules were that we aren't allowed to use a computer or books. We need to talk to our families to figure out as much as we could. The person who figured out the most would get a secret prize at the end of the day tomorrow.

There was also a catch to all of this...not only did we have to make our own family tree, we had to give a whole presentation on it! Sure, it only had to be five minutes long, but any time limit is too long for a presentation.

I did get some clues about Ms. Skele today, though. She decided to give us some parts of her family tree so that we would know how to do this project. At first, I was ready to get excited, but then she mentioned that she didn't know who her real family was because she was adopted when she was younger, so she just based it off of that family. I didn't think that was fair, but kids don't get anywhere by questioning teachers...they don't get anywhere, except for summer school.

Ms. Skele gave out names that meant nothing to me, but she did give some death dates for her family members. The thing is, some died rather recently, and some died a long time ago, but there was no way to tell how old they were when they died, so there was no way to tell how old Ms. Skele was. I'll keep these dates in mind, though. They might come in handy later.

Day Six: Presentation Day

Dear Diary,

I talked to my parents last night and even called my grandma to get as much information as possible about my family tree. While working on it, I found out that I had a great-great-grandpa who was also named Ugh, which I thought was pretty cool. I even wrote down all of the names that I got on a little drawing of a tree that I made. If anything got me some bonus points in this class, I'm sure that it be that drawing.

My mom was pretty excited to see how hard I was working on this project. I told her that I was only doing it for the bonus surprise so that I could win. She didn't really care about my reasoning. She was just proud of me for actually doing my homework. She actually said it like, "It's nice that you're doing your homework for once." It was a backhanded compliment, but I'll take any sort of compliment at this point.

When I got to school I gave my presentation and managed to make it last for 5 minutes and 15 seconds, which meant that I got an A on the project. I got to sit back and listen to the histories of all of the other kid's family stories too. Some of them were pretty interesting. One kid had a shock when he realized that a pigman and a zombie had gotten married and had kids a while back, which was why he was a zombie pigman now.

I didn't end up winning the prize, though. There was a girl in my class who's mom did this sort of thing for a living, so she had her family tree going back hundreds of years. Her prize was an actual sapling that she could grow into a tree. I thought it was kind of funny. Maybe Ms. Skele has a sense of humor after all.

Anyway, the weekend starts tomorrow, and I am SO ready for a break.

Day Seven: Life at Home

Dear Diary,

There's no school today, but also nothing to do. I'm going to hang out with Grunt tomorrow, but I don't have any homework to do, so I just sit and watched TV for most of the day. My mom said at the beginning of summer school that I had to write in this diary every day or else I'd be grounded even when school started back up, and I wasn't about to risk that. Mom hasn't been reading my diary entries because she's been really cool about respecting my privacy when it comes to this diary. She just checks to see that there are words written down, but she takes off her glasses so that she can't actually read what I write in here.

I guess since I don't have anything else to write about, I can write about what my family is like. I guess I already talked about my mom a little bit, but I also have a dad and an older brother. There's a lot to talk about with those two.

My dad is a little bit older than my mom, but he's not a super old guy. I don't even know if he's a doctor or a scientist because he works at a hospital, but he does a lot of Frankenstein sort of stuff. Basically, sometimes zombies lose their limbs and my dad helps to find them new ones. It's actually pretty cool stuff, but I don't think that I could ever have a job like that. It sounds like it would be pretty gross. Sure, there have been some take your kid to work days, but so far I've been able to make up an excuse for all of them.

My brother is a few years older than

me, and he's a bit of a trouble-maker. His name is Roarbert because he used to roar a lot when he was a baby. Originally his name was Carl, but my parents changed it when he was really little because they just didn't think that it fit him. Roarbert and I don't get along very well. He's one of those older brothers who tries to act like he's too cool to spend time with his baby brother. Of course, when a holiday or birthday comes around he'll soften up and spend some extra time with me, so I guess that's cool.

My family isn't all that exciting, so I guess that's all I'll write for today. I'm sure that I'll have more to write about tomorrow after the great time that I'm going to have with Grunt tomorrow.

Day Eight: My Pal, Grunt

Dear Diary,

    I promised that I would write all about my friend, Grunt, so now I'm going to. Grunt is a zombie like me, and he's a few months older than me, but we're still in the same grade. We even got held back together in first grade. I think that's what really made our friendship so solid. We almost got help back together in third grade too, but our teacher just passed us so that she wouldn't need to deal with us for another year. In case I haven't made it clear enough already, Grunt's not the

40

sharpest tool in the box, but he's not so slow that he's annoying to be around. He's a lot like me. He could do his work, but he doesn't. A lot of the time we don't do our homework together. It's like having a study session together, only the exact opposite of that. More like a do-anything-but-study session. They're always fun.

What else can I say about Grunt? He's a pretty cool guy. When we were younger we played with toys, but now that we're a little older we play video games. Sometimes we take hikes or go down to the lake when it's warm at night. We're really great friends, but I guess that we have to be because neither of us really have any other friends because of all of the trouble we make in school. It's our own faults, really, but it doesn't matter so long as we can talk to each other.

Today while I was at his house we talked a lot about what summer school was like. Grunt was mainly complaining about Ms. Skele. I spent a lot of my time complaining about the other kids in the class, though. They were the really annoying ones. They were there because they didn't know the difference between a map of a country between the map of the whole world. I hated to be surrounded by people like that. If anything encourages me to move up a grade it'll just be so that I'm not surrounded by them anymore.

Anyway, I've got to go back to school tomorrow. I wonder what Ms. Skele and my classmates will have in store for me then.

Day Nine: A New Lesson

Dear Diary,

There I was, back to the old grind again...school. I'm starting to think that teachers make out summer school to be way worse than it actually is so that kids will be scared into not doing their homework. I mean, I've been at the summer school for a whole week, and I've only had one homework assignment to do. I can't imagine that I'll have a lot more homework in this class either. I mean, besides the annoying little fact that my only free days are weekends this summer;

this whole summer school thing isn't really that bad. I mean, I'll do what I can to avoid it next year, but I'm not totally upset that I'm stuck here this year.

Today Ms. Skele started a lesson on the Skeleton Wars. From what she mentioned, the Skeletons Wars were a yearly tradition that started around Halloween every year and carried on until either the normal Skeletons or the Wither Skeletons gave up. The winner would get to live in the Overworld and the losers would have to stay in the Nether. I guess that the normal Skeletons won all of the time. They won so often that eventually the Wither Skeletons just gave up and there was never another Skeleton War again.

Whoa, did I really just write all of that? Did I actually take notes? I'm not sure that I've ever done that before. Maybe this summer school thing is really starting to get to me. Then again, this war stuff is a little interesting. I was a little bored, yeah, but how could a person be completely bored by war stories? Just the way that Ms. Skele told the story... it almost sounded like she had been there when it was happening.

Anyway, we're going to learn about basically the same thing tomorrow, but Ms. Skele says that she has a surprise in store for us. I wonder what it could be! Hopefully, it's not a pop quiz...

Day Ten: My History Teacher was a Soldier?

Dear Diary,

Class today was...something else. Usually, teachers seem to teach things because they think that the subject is cool or because they want summers off. Ms. Skele actually taught the subject that she had been involved with in years before. It might not make sense to say that my history teacher was actually a part of history, but with how old that Ms. Skele was, it wasn't actually that hard to imagine.

Today Ms. Skele told us that she was a soldier in the last skeleton war. Apparently, in the early years of the war women weren't allowed to fight because all of the generals in the army thought that girls wouldn't be able to fight as well as boys. Later, a girl went into the army disguised as a boy and ended being the best soldier that the Overworld Skeletons had ever seen. Ever since that girl left the army, all girls were allowed to fight if they wanted to.

Our teacher was one of the women who joined the army. Apparently, the Overworld Skeleton kicked so much butt during that war that there was never another Skeleton War again. It was super cool to hear about history from someone who was actually there.

The only lame part about all of this is that we don't get to hear more about it tomorrow. Tomorrow we need to look up stuff on our own in the library. I think I want to investigate Ms. Skele's story some more. There might be something more than what she's telling us...

Day Eleven: Research Day

Dear Diary,

Today is research day, which means that everyone in the class gets to look deeper into one thing that Ms. Skele has mentioned these last couple of days. I asked Grunt what he was going to do for his research project, and he said that he was looking up the great generals in the early years of the Skeleton War because he liked the idea of some big tough guys telling everyone what to do. I decided to research what Ms. Skele said that she did to find out if it was actually true or not. At

49

least, that's how I told it to Grunt. I didn't want him to think that I was some sort of teacher's pet or something. I told him that I thought Ms. Skele's story was cool, not that I thought she was cool. I mean, she was a teacher, after all.

I got into the library and went straight to the historical biography section. I figured that if Ms. Skele's story was true, then some other famous army person would have to have mentioned her. While I was looking for stuff on the war and people who were in it, I actually found a biography about Ms. Skele! The book was written over a hundred years ago and the pages were loose. I was a little afraid that they were going to fall out. I had to be super careful.

I looked inside of the book until I found the chapter about the Skeleton War. I guess that Ms. Skele's life used to be so exciting that the war was only one chapter of all of the cool stuff that she did. From what I read, it turns out that Ms. Skele joined the army as soon as she was able to.

Within four years (which added up to four wars) she had worked her way up to being second-in-command because she was an expert arrow sniper. She could shoot enemies that were a thousand feet away with just the flick of her bow. She was even nicknamed "the invisible arrow" because no one ever saw her coming. She really was one of the coolest soldiers that the army ever had. She would have been in charge the next year of the war, but that's when the Skeleton Wars ended for good.

With all of my research done, I can be sure that Ms. Skele was telling the truth. Now all I need to do is figure out what to do with what I've learned.

Day Twelve: Another Assignment

Dear Diary,

    Today Ms. Skele was out sick. How does a Skeleton get sick, anyway? That doesn't make any sense. Maybe she broke a bone or something. I don't know. The point is that we had a substitute teacher today. I thought it was a little funny that there were even subs for summer classes, but I guess even subs need to work in the summer sometimes. The substitute's name was Mr. Cemetery, and he was a Zombie like me.

Mr. Cemetery tried to teach us more about the war, but his voice sounded so boring that I could hardly stay awake. The only way I managed not to fall asleep was to pass notes to Grunt the whole time. There wasn't much on those notes that I could write in here, just in case my mom did get around to actually reading the entries. I did draw some funny pictures of Mr. Cemetery being stuck in the mud at a graveyard, asking kids to help him out while they were all too busy napping to help him out. When I write it down it doesn't sound as funny as it actually looked, but when Grunt saw it he laughed so loud that it woke up a couple of the kids who were sitting next to him.

At the end of class, Mr. Cemetery handed out an assignment that was due tomorrow. We had to write an essay about what we would have done if we had to fight in the Skeleton Wars. Man, do I have an idea for this! Wait, do I? Looks like my night will be busy...busy with homework.

Day Thirteen: What Would I Do?

Dear Diary,

    I was a little busy writing my paper today, so I just decided to glue my paper in my diary. I hope my mom doesn't notice that I didn't actually write anything new. This paper is actually pretty good, if I must say so myself, so I might as well throw it in here. Here it goes...

Ugh Zombieton

History Class

What would I do in the Skeleton War?

If I were in the Skeleton War, assuming that I was a Skeleton, I would do the best that I could to fight. I would want to be sneaky about the way that I fought the Wither Skeletons. Like the stories about the girl soldier who disguised herself as a boy to win the war. Since I'm already a boy, I think I would like to disguise myself as a Wither Skeleton so that I could act as a spy.

When I was a spy, I would sneak into the Wither Skeleton camp and pretend that I was joining their side of the army. While I was on the other side of the army, I would do my best to pretend that I was totally into the other side's ideas, but then I would actually write down everything that I learned and send it back to my real camp. Then, once my real camp knew what the other camp was planning, they could attack before the bad guys could get to them.

I wouldn't do much actual fighting if I was in the Skeleton War, but I would still do my best to help my team. I know that the Overworld Skeletons deserved to win the war because they had the best plans to help the Overworld instead of hurt it, and that's why I would be a spy in the Skeleton War.

Day Fourteen: Nerd?

Dear Diary,

    Today in school I turned in my paper and started to talk to Grunt about what I wrote about. Personally, I thought that being a spy in the army would be really cool, but Grunt didn't exactly agree with what I had to say.

    "You actually took this homework seriously? You could have just said that you would have been a soldier that just sat around shooting arrows all day. That's what I wrote, anyway." Grunt said.

"You didn't take this seriously?" I was a little shocked to hear that he didn't put much effort into his homework. Actually...coming from Grunt, it wasn't surprising at all. "The substitute teacher gave us a kind of cool assignment. It's not like we were doing math or anything. It's just like writing a small story or something."

"Wait...are you trying to tell me that you actually had fun doing your homework?" Grunt asked me this like he was personally offended by something I did that didn't even affect him.

"What's wrong with actually doing my homework?" I was starting to get upset with Grunt. I mean, why did he even care if I did my homework or not. Kids were supposed to do their homework. "What's your deal today, anyway?" I was getting mad at him when he said that. I couldn't believe that my own friend was talking to me like this. He had no right! What did I do to him?

"What's wrong is that you never used to do your homework, and now ever since Ms. Skele started teaching here you've been acting like--"

"What have I been acting like?" I yelled at him. "Tell me!"

"You've been acting like a huge NERD!" I was shocked to hear Grunt say this. I used to call other people nerds. Now did the other kids think that I was a nerd? I couldn't bear to talk to Grunt anymore. Instead, I just went home. I need to talk to someone about this, but who?

Day Fifteen: A Second Opinion

Dear Diary,

There's no way that I'm a nerd, it just can't be true. Me, a nerd? That's like saying that Endermen would make the perfect house pet. It just doesn't make sense in either scenario. I'm cool, and Endermen belong in the wild; these are just facts that everyone should know by now. Grunt was wrong. There was no other explanation for what happened yesterday. I needed to talk to someone who knew me better than Grunt. I had to talk to my brother.

I knocked on Roarbert's door and asked him if I could talk to him for a minute. He let me in, but he didn't seem happy about it. He was in the middle of his favorite video game. It was basically illegal for anyone to talk to Roarbert while he was in the zone. He must have known that what I had to say was important if he was willing to let me in. "Roarbert, the other day Grunt called me a nerd just because I was starting to do my homework and because I think the class is kind of cool. Do you think he's right? Am I turning into a nerd?"

Roarbert didn't say anything for a long time. I almost thought that he hadn't even heard me over his loud game. "Liking something in school doesn't make you a nerd. What does being a nerd even mean? If it just means that you're smart, then you're a nerd. If it means that you do school stuff for fun all of the time, then you're not a nerd. If you like your class, but also like skateboarding and stuff, then you're probably not a nerd. Does that answer your question?"

What Roarbert said made sense. If anything, I was just a little bit of a nerd. Maybe I could live with that. I thanked Roarbert and I left him alone to finish his game.

For the rest of the day, I felt a lot better. It was nice to talk to Roarbert. Maybe I just need to embrace this new part of my personality. Who knows? It might even be good for me.

Day Sixteen: Inspired by a Dream

Dear Diary,

    I was really all about embracing my nerdy side, but last night I had a dream that changed everything. In my dream, I was the nerdiest nerd that I've ever seen in my whole life. I was wearing super thick glasses and I was wearing...a sweater vest. Even though I was a fashion disaster, that wasn't even the worst part. Grunt walked into the classroom, and he looked super cool. He was even wearing sunglasses indoors. Ignoring the outfits, Grunt was being a huge jerk in my dream. He was just making a lot of jokes about me being a nerd. Eventually, the whole class chimed in and started making jokes and laughing at me. Even Ms. Skele joined in! I woke up feeling all sweaty. It was gross.

There's no way that I was going to let my dream come true, so before school, I dressed in my coolest clothes and left my pencil at home...on purpose. When school finally started I swaggered into the classroom like I was the coolest kid there, which I was.

During class, I didn't pay attention to a single thing that Ms. Skele said. I'm not sure that she noticed, but I know that Grunt noticed. I was passing notes to Grunt throughout the whole class period and even launched some spitballs at the back of Ms. Skele's skull. Luckily, no one called me out for it, so I didn't get in trouble.

By the end of the school day, I had shown everyone that I was still cool and that I was anything but a nerd. Who knew

that I could save my reputation in one day?
Wait, that's right, I did.

Day Seventeen: You're Only in Trouble if You Get Caught

Dear Diary,

My reign as the King of Cool continued today. Who needs to pay attention in school when you've got swag like me? That's what I've always thought.

Running a kingdom as awesome as mine takes a lot of hard work and attention to detail. There are a few rules that I live by to try to stay as cool as possible. I've decided to write them down for historical purposes. It's something for people to remember me by when I'm a real king instead of just a king of the classroom.

Walk the walk, and talk the talk. Dress cool, say cool things, and act cool.

Don't talk to the nerds. This will only ruin a cool person's reputation and make the nerd think that they could one day be as cool as the cool person talking to them.

Pull pranks as often as possible. What's just as good as good looks and charm? Humor. If someone doesn't have the first two things, then they can always rely on a good joke to make them seem cool.

Don't get caught! This is the most important of all of the rules. Being cool is a hard job to do, and a lot of the job requires the cool person to get in trouble every once in a while. However, getting caught doing something is the opposite of cool. It's lame.

I wrote these rules as part of what will make me famous one day, but also because I broke one of these rules today. I got caught by Ms. Skele. I was sitting in class and drawing in my textbook (which now has every president wearing sunglasses doodled in) and Ms. Skele called on me to answer the question. I knew that I wasn't paying attention, and neither did she, so I wasn't about to pretend that I was. Instead, I answered, "I don't know. You're the teacher, answer it yourself." This highly offended Ms. Skele, which caused her to make me stay inside during break time.

Luckily, since I am the coolest kid around, my getting kept inside actually made kids think that I was cooler than ever before because of my rebellious answer. My coolness is now the highest it's ever been.

If I could send one message to my class it would be, "Watch out subjects, the King of Cool is here to stay, rule, and rock your minds!"

Day Eighteen: An Uprising in the Kingdom of Cool

Dear Diary,

An amazing king should be able to inspire his subjects to be just as great as he is. He should be well respected and honored. He should NOT have competition from a bunch of nerds who are trying to steal his thunder! To explain my little rant, the whole class is trying to act like me now, even the nerdy kids. I mean, that's just not okay. For one, it makes me look average instead of cool. Secondly, everyone is being really mean to

Ms. Skele now. It was funny when I was the only one doing it, but now everyone is grouping up on her and it's really not cool.

I can't even count the number of spitballs that were launched at Ms. Skele today. The whole classroom got really gross and covered in the stuff. Since Ms. Skele couldn't tell who was making the spitballs, everyone had to stay inside during the break time and write an apology letter to her. Sadly, more than one person just made their letter into more spitballs...which just doubled the amount of spitballs that got launched at her.

When it was time to go home I could almost swear that I could see her crying, which made me feel really bad for what I had done. After all, I had encouraged all of this. I'm starting to think that being cool isn't all that it's cracked up to be...

Day Nineteen: Role Reversal

Dear Diary,

A lot of the kids in my class were still being mean to Ms. Skele today, and I couldn't help but think that it was all my fault for trying to be cool again. I was starting to get really sick of all of the kids picking on her. I mean, she literally did nothing to deserve it. I couldn't help what I did today. I just snapped.

So, there I was, it was the middle of class and Ms. Skele was lecturing on something that I was only half paying attention to. Other kids were busy passing notes, throwing paper airplanes, and talking over her lecture. I mean, if they were just napping during class that would be one thing, but they were actively trying to make Ms. Skele's job harder than it had to be, and that just wasn't right.

I decided to do the only thing that I could think of doing. I had to stand up for my teacher. "EVERYONE JUST SHUT UP!" I yelled. My voice echoed around the classroom. I thought that Ms. Skele was going to yell at me for yelling, but the whole classroom was entirely quiet. Usually, I would have just stayed seated and remained silent, but I figured that this was my time to shine.

"Everyone needs to stop this! Ms. Skele is trying to do her job! If you don't want to be here and pay attention, then leave!" I yelled again, and I expected everyone to get up and leave, but instead they just sat there. Ms. Skele got back to teaching.

After class, I expected that Ms. Skele would ask me to stay after class, but she didn't. I guess my unplanned freak out really helped the class. Now I just need to wait to find out if it's going to last.

Day Twenty: Look, but Don't Touch

Dear Diary,

Today's class was a little more interesting than usual, and it wasn't because some kids were fooling around and carving gross pictures into their desks. Ms. Skele had everyone's attention, and she didn't need to yell at the class to get it. Everyone thought the lesson was really cool today because it was just so real. I'll just write it: Ms. Skele brought in totally real artifacts from all of her adventures in her hundreds of years of being part of the living dead.

The artifact that I thought was the coolest was a bow and arrow that she used when she was in the army. The bow was so old that we weren't allowed to touch it, but the arrows that she had were much newer, probably because once a Skeleton shoots an arrow they aren't likely to get it back.

Another cool thing she had was a shield. Until now, I didn't even know that Skeletons used to have shields. Ms. Skele actually planned her whole lesson for the day around it. She told us that Skeletons in the front of the army would use shields so that they, and the Skeletons behind them, would be safe. If a Skeleton in the front of the army made it to the next battle, they would get to go farther back in the line. Basically, the more experienced that the soldier was, the farther away from danger they were. At first, I thought it was silly that they did this because the best soldiers basically got to chill until the best soldiers from the other side got to them. Later I realized that it made total sense to keep the best guys safe.

The one person who didn't seem to learn anything or even care about what was going on was Grunt. He hasn't talked to me since I yelled at the class, and I'm not going to be the one to talk to him first. Maybe it's about time that I start to make new friends...friends that actually care about whether or not they can get into middle school.

Day Twenty-One: My New Friend, Snow

Dear Diary,

As it turns out, making new friends isn't as hard as I thought it would be. Yesterday I made a mental note of a few of the kids in my class that I thought would make good friends. I'm still ignoring Grunt, and I plan to keep ignoring him until he's done ignoring me. I know that might now make a lot of sense, but that's just what I'm going to do.

Anyway, my new friend's name is

Snow. She's a Skeleton. She's not really a slow learner and she's not a slacker. It turns out that she just moved into the school year at a weird time, fell behind, and was never really able to catch up. I thought it was weird that I hadn't noticed her during the school year, but my class was pretty big and most Skeletons looked pretty much the same, so there was that...

Anyway, I talked to Snow in the first place because I remembered that she gave a really cool presentation when we had to learn about our family trees. It turned out that one of her old relatives was in the Skeleton Wars too, and I wanted her to tell me more about it. It also turned out that she didn't know any more than what she wrote in her report, but she said that I could come to her house sometime and hang out to learn more from her parents. I said, "That would be great!" I meant it too.

I might start hanging out with Snow more and with Grunt less if he doesn't change his attitude. I need positive friends in my life, not ones who won't even talk to me. Grunt? Grunt who? If he doesn't talk to me soon I'm sure that I'll forget about him because I'll be too busy hanging out with my cooler friends, my better friends... This thing is going to make Grunt so jealous; I just know it.

Day Twenty-Two: More about Skeletons

Dear Diary,

Today I decided that I wanted to learn a little more about Skeletons. I took Snow up on her offer and visited her house to learn more about where she and her family came from. Things went pretty good the whole time that I was at her house. Snow's mom was very open to answering all of the questions that I had about Skeletons and where they came from.

I asked Snow's mom where Skeletons come from. She told me that a Skeleton could spawn pretty much anywhere in the Overworld, it just had to be dark enough. If they spawned in the Nether then there would be a pretty good chance that they would just be Wither Skeletons. "That's how you can tell the difference of where someone is from, normal Skeletons are pretty much always from Overworld," Snow's mom told me.

Her mom also told me that not all normal Skeletons are the same, either. Apparently, there is a kind of Skeleton called a Stray Skeleton that comes from really cold places. From what I understand, they come from pretty much only icy places, like the ice plains, ice plains spikes, and ice mountains. These skeletons are basically the same as normal Skeletons, except for the fact that they fight differently. They make these wicked arrows that slow down whatever they hit, making it easier for the Stray Skeletons to get to them. Now I know to do my best not to tick off one of them.

I guess that if Skeletons are really careful they can live to be as old and older as Ms. Skele. They can do this because they're dead before they're spawned, so they can't die of illnesses or anything. They only die in wars and other battles, which is a pretty hardcore way to go out anyway.

Tomorrow I'm going to ask Ms. Skele about Zombies. It was cool to learn about Skeletons, but now I'm curious as to where Zombies come from. With a topic his interesting, I'm sure Ms. Skele won't be able to disappoint!

Day Twenty-Three: Zombie Lesson

Dear Diary,

I wanted to ask Ms. Skele about Zombies because I figured that she was old enough to know everything about them. Besides, I didn't really want to talk to my parents about this because I figured they would just be awkward about it.

Anyway, Ms. Skele was a little annoyed that I got her off topic, but I think that I learned more from asking her about Zombies than I would have if she just taught whatever it was that she had planned to teach today.

Today I learned that Zombies, like most other mobs, spawn to make more of themselves. Most Zombies look like me, like a person, but a living-dead person. Sometimes Zombie Villagers spawn, which is just exactly what they sound like. Not all Zombie Villagers come from being spawned, though. Some Zombie Villagers were once normal Villagers that were turned into Zombies after being attacked by a Zombie! This mostly happened years ago. Now Zombie attacks are rare because Zombies are pretty chill mobs. Anyway, the ones that do get turned can be turned back by eating a golden apple. I can't turn into a human though because I'm not part Villager and I just spawned this way.

Just like there are Stray Skeletons, there are also Husk Zombies. The big difference is that the Stray Skeletons come from icy places, while Husk Zombies come from desert biomes. These Zombies are usually gray instead of green, but they look and act pretty much the same as normal Zombies.

That's pretty much all I learned today. It was some pretty interesting stuff, and I hope that I can keep learning more stuff like this when I make it to middle school. Ms. Skele said that she'll give her lesson that she was going to give today tomorrow instead. She said that it's going to be really cool. I guess I'll just have to wait to find out.

Day Twenty-Four: The Many Adventures of Ms. Skele

Dear Diary,

It turns out that I actually interrupted a lesson that would have been just as cool as learning about Zombies yesterday. Ms. Skele didn't really have a lesson plan, though, more or less like a question and answer session with the class. She said that she wanted to do this because the class was almost over, so she wanted to make sure that she taught us everything she could. She handed every kid a piece of paper and said that we could each write down one question. She said that she would answer everyone's question, as long as it was school appropriate.

A lot of the kids questions were stuff like, "Did the Wither Skeletons ever win a battle?" They did, but they never won a war. "How many grandchildren do you have?" None, she was never married. "When was the last Skeleton War?" It was over a hundred years ago. Most of the questions were stuff like that. Most were about what we learned in the last few weeks, and a few were personal.

Eventually, she got to my question, which was the best of all of them as far as I cared. "What other adventures did you go on?" This question made Ms. Skele very talkative, but I think the rest of the class enjoyed her answer.

"I've been around for a while, so I've done a little bit of everything. I fought in that last Skeleton War. When the war was over, I decided to work at a hospital to help soldiers who got hurt in the old wars and who couldn't heal. I did a lot of other things once there was no one else to heal, like teaching, like I'm doing now. I traveled all over Overworld and even in the Nether for a while just to see where I liked to live the most. One of my favorite places was the desert biome, and I met a lot of interesting people there. I liked this place the best, though. I liked teaching the most out of all of my jobs, and now I'm doing that."

I hope that when I'm older I'll get to travel and do a bunch of different jobs. It's cool that Ms. Skele can do whatever she wants to. I hope that I can do that when I grow up too. I never thought that I would want to be as cool as a teacher. It's a little funny when I think about it. Before summer school started I disliked all of my teachers, and now I want to be like one. Things couldn't possibly be more backward. It's actually kind of nice.

Day Twenty-Five: The Last Assignment

Dear Diary,

Today's class went pretty well. I think that everyone is tired out from the long few weeks that we've had in this history class. The whole class really learned a lot so far. I've even been getting all A's and B's on all of the assignments so far, so unless I don't even do the next project, I'm going to pass this class. I'll be one step closer to passing the fifth grade and getting into middle school.

I'm actually starting to worry about whether or not Grunt is going to be able to pass this class. He's been doing all of his homework, but he's also been being really lazy about it. If he doesn't get at least a C on this next assignment, then he might not be able to pass the class. Even though we're in the middle of not talking to each other right now, I still hope that we can get into middle school together.

I've been talking about this assignment for so long, but I guess I never actually mentioned what the homework assignment was. Ms. Skele wants everyone to pick some historical period, any one of them that we know a lot about and write about what we would be like if we lived back then. It's kind of like the Skeleton War assignment, but this time, we can pick whatever time period we want. Ms. Skele is letting us pick what we want because she thinks that it will be more fun this way. I don't know what I want to write about, but I better pick something soon because the paper is due tomorrow. Anyway, I've got to get writing!

Day Twenty-Six: The Dark Ages

Dear Diary,

For my paper, I decided to write about the dark ages. During that time, a lot of humans and Villagers didn't even think that Zombies were real. When they did see a Zombie, they thought it was just a sick person. They would take in the Zombie, but then the Zombie would infect others. That's really how some of the world's biggest plagues happened. Anyway, I wanted to write about this time period basically because I thought it would be cool. I copied the paper here in my diary just for fun.

If I lived as a dark ages Zombie I would live in a creepy coffin underground. If I lived there, I would be protected from the sunlight during the day, At night, I would break out of my coffin and walk around Overworld. I wouldn't actually want to infect anyone, though. I would do my best to avoid humans and just hang out with other mobs instead.

Since a lot of the other mobs were fought all of the time back in the day, I would want to be there to help them out. I would be there to help them protect themselves against whatever might come at them. Since it was in the dark ages, I would be able to use an old rusty sword to fight my enemies.

Basically, if I lived in the dark ages, I would do whatever I could to keep things pretty light. I would do my best to help my kind and avoid trouble with every other mob. If I could do all of these things, I think that the dark ages wouldn't be as dark as they were in real life.

I think this paper was pretty good, but I won't know for sure until tomorrow when I get my grade back. If I pass this paper I'll pass this history class and then I'll be one step closer to getting into middle school!

Day Twenty-Seven: The Last Day of History Class

Dear Diary,

Today is the last day of this class. I don't really know how I feel about it. I thought that this class was going to be totally lame, but it turned out to be a lot better than I ever would have expected it to be. It was...cool. Ms. Skele said that she had a surprise for all of us. For a second, I worried that it was a last minute pop quiz, but she really just pulled out a cake that she had made herself just for our class.

Ms. Skele said that today was going to be a party day to celebrate the end of class. She said that everyone who took a class had passed! I was thrilled to hear that I had been able to pass the class. She passed back my report card, and I got a B+ in the class. That's the best that I've ever done in a class. When I saw the report I couldn't help but yell out, "I'm slightly above average!" Everyone laughed. I wonder if that means that Ms. Skele is a great teacher if I' becoming a better student or both.

Since she said that everyone passed I knew that Grunt was going to go to the next class. I didn't talk to him today, but I'm glad that we're moving on together. I'd be pretty bummed if my best friend couldn't move on with me. I flashed him a thumb's up before I left. He smiled. I wonder if that means he's done being mad at me. I guess I just need to wait to find out.

Day Twenty-Eight: Grunt's Grunting

Dear Diary,

I woke up early in the night because someone was knocking loudly on my bedroom door. I let out a loud "ggrr!" as I got up. Why was someone waking me up so early in the night? School didn't start back up for a few more days. I slowly got out of bed, and not just because Zombies do most things slowly, and opened my door. I was surprised to see Grunt on the other side of it.

"What are you doing here?" I asked

him. I wasn't mad that he woke me up anymore. I was just surprised to see him here this early in the night.

"Your mom let me in. I just wanted to talk to you." He looked like he was waiting for an answer from me, but I didn't know what to say. We hadn't talked in a while, and I wasn't exactly sure what to open up with. Since I didn't know what to say, Grunt just starting ranting. "I feel really badly about how we haven't been talking. It wasn't cool of me to call you a nerd. You just know how I feel about school. Sometimes I feel silly and lose my cool. I'm sorry."

I had never heard Grunt apologize and mean it before. Whenever he said sorry before it was because his mom told him to, but I could tell that he really meant it this time. "Thanks," was all that I could think to say back to him.

"Can we go back to talking and being friends?"

"Yeah!" I yelled. This was the next best news that I got after hearing that I passed the history class. "Let's make up for lost time," I suggested and Grunt grunted in agreement.

We spend the rest of the night at the park. We had a great time. I'm glad that I have my best friend back.

Day Twenty-Nine: Next on the Schedule...

Dear Diary,

The science part of my summer school is going to start on Monday next week, which means that I'm in the middle of my only week off. I think that the school only gives us time off just to give the new teachers time to set up their lessons or whatever. I don't really care what it's for. All I care about is that I have a little more time to hang out with my friends.

Today I introduced Snow to Grunt. Of course, they had actually met first in our summer school class, but they had never hung out before. We went to the local graveyard and pretended that we were back in the old days when Zombies turned humans. We took turns being the humans and the Zombies. It was actually a pretty fun game. It also reminded me a lot of some of Ms. Skele's old lessons. I wasn't really expecting it, but they got along really well. I think this means that the three of us will start hanging out a lot more often. It would be really cool to add one more person to our group of friends.

I hope that we can all stay friends during the next section of the summer school program. It would be great to have the two of them by my side the whole time. If they were all near me, then I know that every moment would have something cool about it. Thinking about all of this stuff actually makes me a little excited about summer school. It's weird. At the beginning of the month I never would have thought that I would be thinking that summer school could be fun, but now here I am, writing that exact thing down. The whole world seems backward, but it also feels pretty good. I think this could be the start of something great.

Day Thirty: The Letter

Dear Diary,

Today I got a letter in the mail, or well, my parents got a letter in the mail about me. It said that I had made it to the next class, which I already knew. It said that I would be taking a science class, which I also already knew. What I didn't know before was that Ms. Potionbrewer was going to be the one teaching our class.

Ms. Potionbrewer was a witch mix that lived outside of my village. Usually, my school didn't let witches in, but they were letting in her because of how great of a teacher she was. I heard that she grew up as a witch, but went to an all- monster's college to learn how to teach. At least, that's what my mom said when she saw her name on the paper.

I wonder what it will be like to be taught by a witch... I wonder if she'll be as cool as Ms. Skele, but I doubt that she'll be able to be that cool. Even if the class is lame, I'm sure that I'll have a great time with Grunt by my side again. I even heard that the Skeleton girl that I made friends with is going to be in the class too. With my old and new friends there, I'm sure that class will be a little fun, even if the teacher is boring. I guess all that I can do now is wait to see what happens. All I know is that it'll have to be magical to have a witch as a science teacher

Book 2: My Science Teacher is A Witch

Day One: My History Teacher was a Skeleton

Dear Diary,

My name is Ugh, and the word 'ugh' pretty much sums up how I feel about this summer so far. I may have messed around a lot during the school year, and by messing around I mean that I skipped a lot of classes. I also didn't turn in most of my homework. My teachers didn't appreciate all of my slacking, which is why I just finished up my first month of summer school and why I'm about to start my second month of it.

Last month I took a history class with my friend Grunt. My friend Grunt is really more of a partner in crime than a friend. He was pretty much always by my side when I skipping class. It's kind of ironic now because we're both stuck in summer school together. Sometimes Grunt and I get mad at each other because I'm to take this thing seriously, but he still wants to fool around. Last month we didn't talk for a while, so I made a new friend named Snow. She's actually pretty cool, even if she's not a slacker.

My history teacher was really cool too. She was a Skeleton who fought in the last Skeleton War. Since then she's done a lot of other cool stuff, and she even brought in some old stuff from her adventures. She really made the class fun. Oh, I don't know if I need to mention it or not, but I totally passed that class. Which means that I have one class down, and only two to go.

My next class is going to be a science class that's taught by a Witch. I have no idea what to expect, so I'm a little nervous about it still. I guess all that I can do about it is to wait. My first day of science class starts tomorrow, so I might as well get ready for it now.

Day Two: The First Day of Science Class

Dear Diary,

I woke up early in the night so that I could get ready for my first day of science class. I didn't know much about science, mostly because I had skipped so many science classes during the school year. I mean, I could learn a lot about science if I wanted to; it's not like I'm dumb or anything. My mom says that I just don't work hard. I won't say this to her, but she's probably right about that.

Anyway, when I got to the school I sat down in the science lab next to Grunt. I was a little surprised that he was here before me. I bet that his parents made him wake up at the crack of dusk since he was pretty close to failing the history class. "What's up?" I asked him as I sat down. I also waved to Snow as she sat in the front row of the class.

"Not much. I'm so tired... I was up until the afternoon yesterday, so I didn't get much sleep this morning. I'm really not looking forward to this class. I would have skipped it, but my mom drove me straight to the front door. She's getting smarter, I'm telling you."

Besides Grunt and Snow, I really didn't know a lot of the other kids in this class. Sure, they had all been in my class during the whole school year, but my class was really big. It probably had a couple hundred kids in it. Most of the monsters in Overworld sent their kids to my school, so it wasn't all that strange that I couldn't remember some people's names. I guess if

I don't know anyone, then I'll have a better chance at making new friends than I would have if I did already know the people here.

We didn't have time to talk much more because the teacher walked in. I had heard that she was a witch, but she wasn't nearly as ugly as most witches were. At least, she was just average. It kind of threw me off guard. She said that she had somewhere to be, so she couldn't actually teach today, but she handed out a list of things that we were going to cover later in the class. All in all, this was definitely the shortest class that I've ever had, and by the look of the teacher, I think that this might end up being the weirdest class that I'll ever take too. I guess that I have the whole month to figure that out, though!

Day Three: Something Called a Syllabus

Dear Diary,

    "Since you are all trying to get into middle school, this class is going to be set up like a middle school class would be." That's how our teacher opened up class today. She also added on, "Get out your syllabus so that we can discuss what we going to learn this month." No one really did anything when she said that, probably because none of us had heard the word 'syllabus' before. "It's the paper that I handed out yesterday before I left," she said, sounding annoyed this time. At least everyone actually knew what she was talking about this time. There was a big classwide "Oh," as everyone took papers out of their bags.

Honestly, I hadn't even read this paper until now, and a syllabus kind of sounded like the worst test imaginable. I was glad to be wrong when I found out that a syllabus was really just a list of things that we were going to have to cover.

Of course, as soon as I looked at the paper I got the same sick feeling that I would have gotten if it had been a test. The syllabus was full of stuff that we would be doing. We had one chemistry lab every week! We had to learn about science stuff on the other days, practice it once a week, and test it once a week! The very end of the class wouldn't be celebrated with a party, but instead with a huge exam! I was starting to feel like this teacher wasn't going to be as cool as Ms. Skele was. Oh, by the way, this teacher's name is Miss Enchantment.

I'm not sure I'll be able to pass this class. It just looks like everything is going to go by too quickly. I wonder if Grunt will be able to pass... I might even have to study if this class gets as crazy as I think it will. Diary, if it's possible, wish me luck for the next month--I'm going to need it!

Day Four: Lab Safety

Dear Diary,

Today Miss Enchantment told everyone that it would be lab safety day. With a name like that, any normal person would have figured that today would have been pretty safe. On the weird side of things, whoever would have thought that would have been wrong.

Things started okay enough. Miss Enchantment handed out goggles to everyone and these big huge rubber gloves. We would have to wear these whenever we were doing any chemistry experiments. We started our first mini experiment today, and it went nothing like Miss Enchantment thought it would go.

We were doing something simple today, just learning how to deal with fire so that we wouldn't melt anything or burn down the classroom later in bigger experiments. Apparently, Miss Enchantment hadn't heard about Kevin. Kevin just happened to be in the science summer school class because he almost burned down the school in the science class during the school year. That was one of the days that I was actually there. It was crazy, but no one got hurt, which was good.

The point is, Kevin was in this class, and he hadn't learned his lesson from last time. All of the other kids were okay with controlling their flames, but within minutes, Kevin's fire was out of control. The flames were higher than everyone else's by a lot. They were so big that they lit the fire safety paper on fire. I thought it was kind of funny, but Miss Enchantment didn't. She threw water on the fire and ended class early.

This class keeps proving me right; this thing really is going to be crazy.

Day Five: The First Real Lab

Dear Diary,

After the whole thing that happened with Kevin yesterday, I would have thought that Miss Enchantment would have decided to quit on having a chemistry lab, but when I showed up today, all of the lab stations had a bunch of stuff next to them. I was 100% ready to yell for Grunt to be my lab partner, but then Miss Enchantment said, "The school has given us enough supplies for everyone to do their own experiment! Isn't that great?!" Miss Enchantment was the definition of excited when she said this, but I was anything else.

Grunt and I still sat at tables that were next to each other, but it was a real bummer to have to work alone. The first thing that we had to do was set up the chemistry equipment. This was probably the hardest part for me. I know that we went over all of this stuff the other day in class, but I was so distracted by the fire that I could hardly remember what I was supposed to do.

Eventually, I was able to figure out how to set up all of the stuff and how to light the fire to heat up the ingredients for the experiment. However, while I was lighting the fire I accidentally caught my instruction paper on fire. I was able to blow it out before Miss Enchantment noticed, but some of the instructions had burned off before I could blow out the fire.

I remembered Miss Enchantment saying that we had to put a bottle of water in the pot, so I did that. There was a bunch of Nether Wart on the table, though. I had no idea how much I was supposed to put into the pot.

I had spent so much time putting together the equipment that I didn't have a lot of time to worry about this. I just threw in all of the Nether Wart that was on the table and called it good. I mean, a lot of it hard fit in the cauldron, but it worked.

Miss Enchantment said that the experiments needed to cook overnight, so we would test them tomorrow. I have a bad feeling about how mine will turn out...

Day Six: Testing the Experiments

Dear Diary,

Today is the day that I got to find out how I did in my experiment. Spoiler alert: it didn't go well.

All of the experiments had cooked throughout the night and now they were ready to be tested by Miss Enchantment. I was nervous right away because my experiment looked a lot different from everyone else's. All of the experiments had been put into clear bottles. Most of the experiments were some shade of blue, and then there was mine...My experiment had turned out brown. It looked almost exactly like mud. I was so embarrassed, but at least no one else knew that it was mine.

The one thing that made me feel better was that Grunt didn't do very well, either. His experiment wasn't brown, but it wasn't blue either. There were a few other kids who had purple experiments. Miss Enchantment looked pretty disappointed at the work that we had turned in. I felt kind of bad for her, actually. I bet she had expected more from us.

Luckily, Miss Enchantment didn't try to talk to me about the work that I had done. I was a little nervous, thinking that she might hold me back after class or something or scold me for my bad work like how my mom scolds me if I don't do my chores the right way.

Well, at least tomorrow is Saturday so that I can have a little break from all of this school stuff. Grunt and I have some plans to hang out tomorrow, so I'm sure that whatever we do will be way more exciting than my failure in class today. I'll write all about it tomorrow.

Day Seven: Grunt's House

Dear Diary,

I'm so glad that I finally get a break from school. I know it only started this week, but it seems like half the month is already over. I mean, I wish that this month was already over. This science class is already so complicated, and with all of the stuff that Miss Enchantment has planned for the month... I just hope that I can keep up. Anyway, now's not the time to think about that stuff. I had a great time with Grunt today, and that'll be way more exciting to write about.

Grunt and I did talk about school for a little while, but that was pretty boring, so the talk didn't last for very long. Eventually, we got onto talking about something a little more exciting. Apparently, Grunt has a crush on one of the girls in our class. There's a girl in this science class that wasn't in the history class that we took last month, but she was in our class during the school year. I guess that Grunt had just started to like her since we started this class.

"She was sitting next to me when we were working in the lab the other day, and she's actually really funny. I think I'm going to bring some extra snacks on Monday to share with her so that she knows I like her."

I thought it was a little weird that Grunt liked a girl since he didn't really seem to like much of anything. Besides, he was like ten years old, what was he supposed to do with a girlfriend? There wasn't even lunchtime in summer school so he couldn't even sit next to her and share some fried brains.

I won't get swept up in this weird love thing he's going through. I half-listened while he told me his great plan to romance this girl, but really, I was more focused on the video game that we were playing. No romance there and no romance in my life either, but I kind of like it that way.

Day Eight: A Call Home

Dear Diary,

Today was going really well. I had the day off of school so I was just sitting in my room playing video games. My parents were in a good mood so they even forgot that I had chores that I was supposed to be doing. This had the potential to be the best day of my summer, but then the phone rang. It wasn't until my mom hung up that I was really in trouble.

My mom walked into my room, unplugged my video games, and stared at me like I had eaten the last known cow. I didn't know why she looked so mad. I guess there was a possibility that I had done something wrong, but I couldn't think of what it might be. Then my mom said those three words that no kid ever wants to hear, "Your teacher called." As soon as Mom said this I knew that I was in trouble. I didn't know why Miss Enchantment would call my parents on a Sunday. All I knew was that it couldn't have been for a good reason.

"Miss Enchantment said that you failed the very first lab that you had. Is this true?" I figured that I hadn't done well, and I guess I could have assumed that I did fail. All I could do to reply was nod because I didn't really know what else to say.

My mom looked relieved to see that even though I was failing I wasn't lying about failing, and that's what really counts, right? "Well, since it's true, I guess I'm going to have to do what she suggested then..."

126

I hated when Mom trailed off like this. I knew she was just trying to bug me. "What did she suggest that you do?" I may have asked this in a really annoyed tone which may or may not have ticked off my mom a little bit.

"She said that she wants you to show up for tutoring with her after class every Monday. I'm going to call her back and tell her that it's okay."

That's when I got really mad. "Mom! Don't do that! I don't need tutoring! It was one mess up!" I wanted to spend as little time as possible in school, not more time.

"Too bad, you need to pass this class to get into middle school, so if your teacher says that you need tutoring, then you need it. We're not going to discuss this anymore." My mom left my room with a huff. It was almost like she was proud of herself for further ruining my summer.

Wait...today is Sunday...which I guess means that my first day of tutoring is

tomorrow... Diary, wish me luck. I'll need
it.

Day Nine: Tutoring

Dear Diary,

When I woke up I was really not looking forward to tutoring. I tried faking sick, but my mom knew that I wasn't actually sick. I would have gotten away with it if I was able to hide the thing I used to make the thermostat hotter than I actually was. Of course, my mom called me out for having her hair dryer in my room, probably because I've never actually used a hair dryer before.

Class today was really lame, too. I

tried to tell Grunt what was up throughout most of the class, but I couldn't actually get my whole message out because Miss Enchantment kept interrupting our conversation by shushing us. She told Grunt, "It's rude to talk while others are talking." He replied in a really brutal way, telling her, "Then quit talking while I'm talking." This made Miss Enchantment get a really angry look on her face, but for whatever reason, Grunt didn't actually get in trouble. It didn't seem fair, but it was still entertaining to watch.

When class was finally over I had to watch as all of the other kids left the room to go home. They looked so happy...so free... I was stuck here. I would have thought that there would be more kids in this tutoring thing, but it was just me. It made me feels really stupid, which is dumb because I wasn't even here because I was stupid. I was here because my instruction paper burnt. I wonder if she would have let me to leave early if I told her that. I probably should have, but I was too embarrassed to admit it.

Miss Enchantment gave me a whole lesson about how it matters how much of something a person puts inside of an experiment. "You can't just put however much of something that you want or else it'll turn out funky," she explained to me. I think she was trying to sound cool by using the word 'funky' which actually made her sound lame.

The whole thing was really pointless. I didn't learn anything the whole time. The only thing that this taught me to do was to do the experiment perfectly next time so that I don't have to put up with this dumb tutoring thing again. I'm going to be the experiment expert. I'll show Miss Enchantment. I'll show everyone!

Day Ten: Talking and Trouble

Dear Diary,

There has been a terrible update on my life. My mom has grounded me during the school week until I can get my grades up. I'm not allowed to hang out with any of my friends Monday-Thursday, and it's really bumming me out. I need to get all of my time in with my friends during school now, which is part of the reason why I'm in even deeper trouble today. I've got to explain this better. Here's what happened in class today.

The class was super boring today. I can't even remember what Miss Enchantment was talking about. I wanted to tell Grunt all about the tutoring that I had to go through yesterday and pretty much just tell him about how boring it was. Miss Enchantment wasn't having this stuff today. She kept shushing us, but Grunt and I aren't the types of guys to get shushed, so we just started ignoring her.

Grunt and I just kept talking, and then Miss Enchantment put both of our names on the board. I don't know why she did that. I mean, usually, teachers stopped doing that after third grade at this school. I don't know what her deal was. Anyway, Grunt kept talking so I kept talking and then Miss Enchantment put a check next to both of our names. What did it mean? That's what I thought to myself, but I didn't care enough to stop talking.

Two checks later she ended class and called my mom and Grunt's dad. We were in big trouble. We were punished with an after class detention on Thursday.

If there was such a thing as double grounded, then that's exactly what I would be right now. My mom is super upset. I need to shape up, or at least learn how to whisper better, if I want to stop getting into trouble. The last thing I need is more tutoring or chores from Mom...

Day Eleven: Another Lab, Another Mistake

Dear Diary,

As cool as lab days might sound...they're actually the worst. I thought that combining all of these different materials to make something new would be the coolest thing that I would ever have to do in school, but it actually isn't very fun at all.

Even though lab day stinks, I know that I need to do my best on these things if I want to get out of tutoring with Miss

Enchantment. So far she seems like a really strict teacher, and I'm not sure that I like her at all. My great pal Grunt didn't seem to think the same way. Well, he knew that he didn't like Miss Enchantment, but he didn't agree with me about doing well in labs.

Basically, today was pretty rough. I did my best to do well in my lab. This one was a lot more complicated than the last one. Even though my instructions didn't catch on fire, this time, it was still hard to do everything right. I did my best, though. However, Grunt did his worst.

There I was, paying close attention to what I was doing, but there Grunt was, doing literally everything wrong. Miss Enchantment even told him what he was doing wrong, and she was even able to fix some of his mistakes, but he just messed it back up again. I knew that he was doing it on purpose, and so did Miss Enchantment.

I have a bad feeling about all of this. If Grunt doesn't shape up he might fail this class, which would mean that he wouldn't get into middle school with me. I might try to talk some sense into him tomorrow, but I'm not sure if I'll be able to no matter hard I try...

Day Twelve: Detention

Dear Diary,

Today is the day...the day that I needed to suffer in detention for a whole hour! This is really lame because the class is usually an hour long, so it's like having a class that's twice as long as normal, but way more than twice as boring. At least I had Grunt there to keep me entertained... Actually, the whole thing might have gone better if Grunt wasn't there. Let me explain.

I was ready to sit around and take a

nap during detention, but Grunt had other plans. Grunt came prepared with only two things, but they were the only two things that he needed to cause problems with Miss Enchantment. In his pockets were one straw and a few pieces of crumpled up paper. It was the perfect weapon and the perfect ammo to really tick off a teacher quickly. Luckily, he didn't involve me this little scheme or else I would have gotten in just as much trouble as he did.

Miss Enchantment told us to sit down, be quiet, and think about what he had done. I was ready to do this, but this is when Grunt decided to put his plan into action. Miss Enchantment sat down to grade the labs from the other day and Grunt pulled out his straw and loaded it with a few spitballs. He launched a few at her, and man did she get ticked.

She didn't yell when she got hit by the spitball. All she said was, "It looks like you'll be seeing me in detention again tomorrow." It was simple but savage.

The rest of the time in detention was really tense, and I was so happy to get out of there when the time was up. I'm going to behave from now on. I do NOT want to go through that awkward silence ever again. Diary, I learned my lesson today, that's for sure.

Day Thirteen: Better and Worse

Dear Diary,

Today is Friday, which means that it's time to test the experiments that the class did the other day. The experiments were supposed to turn out blue again this time, and my experiment didn't turn out to be a gross brown this time. It wasn't blue either...but it was purple, and that was good enough for me! Miss Enchantment even wrote on my paper that I did a lot better this time, even though she does still want me to go to tutoring again on Monday. I think if I do better on my experiment next week then I won't need to go to tutoring anymore. Of course, class will almost be over by then...so I guess I'm almost done with tutoring no matter what happens.

Even though I did a great job on my experiment, Grunt really did a bad job. When my experiment went badly it turned brown, when Grunt's turned out badly it was pitch black. Miss Enchantment seemed really mad that Grunt did so badly, but since she knew that he did it on purpose she didn't make him sign up for tutoring at least not today. Maybe she'll call his parents tomorrow or something. If he doesn't get signed up for tutoring it just won't be fair.

There's something else going on today that just wasn't fair. Grunt got super mad at me because I did well on my experiment when he did badly. He did badly on purpose, and he had expected me to do badly too. I mean, we never even talked about a plan like this. I don't know what his deal is. Grunt just switches up his mind too much when it comes to this stuff.

I had plans to hang out with Grunt tomorrow, but since he's being a jerk and getting mad at me for no reason I canceled and asked if Snow wanted to hang out instead. I might go to her place tomorrow and just hang out with her family. It should still be a good time, especially since she's not a jerk like someone I know...

Day Fourteen: Snow's House

Dear Diary,

I went to Snow's house today and it was great. Her house was totally stress-free and relaxing. I think it was so nice to be there because Snow never gets mad at me without having a good reason. I mean, she did get a little mad when I took the last piece of pizza, but that's totally understandable. I would get mad if someone did that to me. She got over it when I let her have the last piece of cake. I think this is how friendships are supposed to be.

I've been here before and Snow's family was just as great as they were last time that I was here. We watched this really weird movie that was based on crazy art. I'm not even sure what it was about, but it was still pretty good, not that I would watch it again.

I think that we're going to hang out again next weekend even if Grunt is done being mad at me. Maybe we'll all hang out together or something. It would be nice if we could do that, I guess. Until Grunt shapes up, I'm glad that I have a great friend like Snow to fall back on. Now I only wish that Grunt could be a good friend that I could depend on.

I think that I'm going to talk to my brother about this tomorrow. I don't think that friends are supposed to act the way that Grunt does, and all I want it some advice on what to do about it. My brother may not always be the coolest guy, but I know that I can always talk to him when something is wrong. I'll write all about the brotherly advice tomorrow.

Day Fifteen: Roarbert's Brotherly Talks

Dear Diary,

Every once in a while Grunt gets all worked up about something dumb and he takes it out on me. Last month he was upset with me because I was doing well in class and he thought I was being a teacher's pet. Now he's mad at me because he failed his experiment and I didn't. I think he's just worried that I'm way smarter than him or something.

Roarbert isn't always the coolest brother, but I know that I can talk to him about the sort of stuff that really matters, like this. I walked into his room and told him what was going on with Grunt, and Roarbert just replied with a complaint. "Doesn't Grunt get up to this sort of this all of the time? What's his deal?" It sounded like Roarbert was just as annoyed with Grunt as I was. It was kind of nice to see someone else feel the same way that I did.

I told him what I thought Grunt's deal was, but that didn't seem to make Roarbert any more compassionate towards him. "I don't think it matters if he thinks that you're smarter than him or whatever. If he's really your friend then he'll cool off and cheer you on for being so smart, not make you feel bad for it. If he keeps this up then you should just stop being friends with him."

I understood what he said, but I didn't like it. I liked being friends with Grunt when he was in a good mood, but he was hardly ever in a good mood this summer. Maybe I needed some new

147

friends and to do that I might need to get rid of some old friends...

Day Sixteen: More about Miss Enchantment

Dear Diary,

The class was pretty boring today, so I don't really have too much to write about in that area of my life. Grunt was still being dumb, so I didn't want to talk to him. The last thing I needed was to talk to someone who got mad at me all of the time for no reason. Since I wasn't talking to Grunt, I had to pay attention in class, which made everything a lot more boring that it should have been.

My tutoring lesson today was actually kind of cool, even though it was still during school. I got to learn a lot about Miss Enchantment so far. After talking to her and Ms. Skele, I'm starting to learn that not all teachers are just boring or mean. Some of them are actually pretty cool. I wonder if all teachers are secretly really cool...

Anyway, today I learned that most witches didn't grow up to teach other monsters. Most of them stayed behind in their old witch villages and only taught other witches. The other witches went out into different parts of Overworld and made potions, treated people with spells, or spent their lives adventuring doing a little bit of everything. Miss Enchantment was allowed to teach other monsters because she was half human. Her mom was a witch and her dad was a human. Usually, this would have come as a bit of a nasty shock to a normal human, but he knew that she was a witch as soon as he met her, so it wasn't weird.

Miss Enchantment taught all monsters because making potions was pretty much the same thing as doing chemistry, except for without all of the magic. She wanted to do something that brought together both sides of her family.

When she was done telling me about herself and teaching me my lesson she asked what I wanted to be when I grew up, and I told her that I honestly didn't know what I would want to be yet. She said it was okay that I didn't know yet and went back onto tutoring me. Her question has me thinking now. What should I be when I grow up? With all of these cool stories I keep hearing, I might just decide to be a teacher. Wouldn't that be funny? Some summer school kid growing up to teach all-year school. It would be a challenge, but a Zombie like me is up for any challenge!

Day Seventeen: All About Witches

Dear Diary,

In my history class, I got really interested in the history of skeletons and why they existed. After my talk with Miss Enchantment yesterday, I kind of wanted to know more about witches. I decided to ask Miss Enchantment about witches. She agreed to do it because she figured it might help with the class, and the whole class was glad to have the distraction.

Miss Enchantment said that most witches are born as witches, so their parents know to send them to a witches-only school right away so that they can learn to make potions. Some witches weren't born that way, though. Sometimes humans can turn into witches if they're stuck by lightning when they're still kids. I thought that was crazy, but it was still really cool to hear about.

Another weird thing about witches is that they can't hurt each other with potions. I don't know why it works like that, but it's pretty cool to know that it does.

We didn't have any homework today since we didn't actually learn anything about chemistry. I'm not sure what will happen tomorrow, but maybe I'll learn some more, and if I don't I'm sure that I'll have a lot of fun.

Day Eighteen: Another Lab Day

Dear Diary,

I was so prepared for this lab day. I spent a lot of yesterday after school studying measurements that experiments need and what different experiment ingredient can do. My mom even made a cake with me. She said that when she was in school they taught her about chemistry with cooking. I guess a lot of the same things worked in both chemistry and baking cake, which I thought was pretty cool. Anyway, I wanted to do all of this because I want to have a good grade by the time this class is over with. I think this might be the last or second to last lab that we're going to have, and if I do a good job I might not need to have tutoring anymore. Besides my mom will probably get me a new video game or something if I do super well.

When I got to school I wasn't nervous at all about the experiment. I knew that I was prepared for this lab, and I wasn't going to let anything mess me up, especially not Grunt. He was still ignoring me. I did my best to ignore him, but I just couldn't for some reason.

While I worked on my lab I couldn't help but noticed how Grunt was doing on his lab. It didn't look like he was trying to fail this time. It did look like he was struggling to do a good job, though. I started to get worried if he would pass this class. Even though we were in a fight, I didn't want him to fail. I wanted us to go to middle school together, but at this rate, it looked like he would be left behind.

I turned in my lab in and left the classroom. If Grunt doesn't shape up I might have to talk to him. I don't want to... but sometimes a friend's just got to do what a friend's got to do, even if they didn't want to do it at all.

Day Nineteen: The Results

Dear Diary,

Today I got back my grade for my experiment, and it just what I expected! I finally got an A! That means that I don't need to go to tutoring anymore unless I feel like it, and I don't think that I'm going to feel like that anytime soon. My Mondays have gotten a little freer. I wonder what I'm going to do with this extra hour of free time. It's a small thing, but it's so big to me.

I couldn't help but look over to see

what grade Grunt got on his lab. Let me just say that it wasn't a passing grade. I knew that if Grunt failed one more thing that he would fail the whole class. I didn't say anything to him about it. I wasn't sure if it would be rude to mention that he was failing, especially considering that I had to sneak a peek at it instead of asking for his permission to look at it.

I thought about bringing up his grades to Miss Enchantment, but of course, she already knew all about it. I wonder why she wasn't doing anything about it. It was probably because he was really rude to her all of the time. He was being pretty rude to me too, but I think that we were still friends. I wrote about helping him yesterday, but I wimped out about it today. Now that I've seen his grade I know that I need to do something about it.

Tomorrow I'm going to try to talk Grunt into getting himself into tutoring. If he won't go, then I'll tutor him myself if I have to. It'll be hard work, but it'll be worth it if I can help my friend get into middle school. I just need to keep telling myself that I need to do this, or else I'll wimp out again. I need to stay strong for my friend, no matter how hard it might be.

Day Twenty: Trying to Talk

Dear Diary,

I did my best to work up the guts to talk to Grunt about tutoring. I was so busy thinking about this during class that I was hardly paying attention to what Miss Enchantment was talking about. Looking back, I really get distracted when I'm in class. If I didn't study so much I would definitely be failing this class.

By the end of class, I couldn't remember what Miss Enchantment had taught us and I was sick to my stomach at the thought of talking to Grunt. I knew that he wasn't going to take this well, but I knew that I had to do it. I walked up to Grunt after class and told him, "We need to talk." This sounded way harsher than I meant it to, but it at least got Grunt to stop and listen to me.

"What do you want?"

I waited until everyone else was out of the classroom to talk to him about this issue. "I know that you're not going well in class. I think that you should sign up for tutoring. If you don't pass this class you aren't going to get into middle school!" I yelled to convince him.

He yelled back, but I don't think it was to convince me of anything. "I don't need tutoring! I'm not stupid or anything!"

"I was in tutoring, and I'm not stupid. It helped to make me smarter, and I think that you might need it too. I would even go with you if you wanted me to."

Grunt shoved past me without even

looking at me. "I don't need any help, especially not from you." He was too quick for me to catch up to him before his mom came to pick him up.

I had tried to convince him to go into tutoring, but it just didn't work. Should I give up? I'm starting to wonder if it's worth my trouble to help Grunt.

Day Twenty-One: Snow and her Crew

Dear Diary,

     I was in no mood to deal with Grunt today. I tried to help him yesterday and he just shoved past me and ignored everything that I had to say. If he wasn't going to take my friendly advice, then I wasn't going to spend my free time with him, not that he invited me... Anyway, I had time to hang out with Snow today. She wanted me to meet some of her friends, and I'm glad that I got to.

     Snow transferred to our school in

the middle of the year, which is why she's in summer school. Today a few of her friends from her old school came to her house and she wanted me to meet them. Her friends that came up were both skeletons like her. Their names were Amy and Adam. They were really cool, like Snow.

It turned out that Amy was in her school's drama club and she was in all of the school's plays. She even got to play the skull in Hamlet once. Adam wasn't into plays or anything like that; he was much more of a sport's guy. He liked to play soccer more than anything. Once I learned this, I asked him if he wanted to play a game of it, so he and I were on a team against Amy and Snow.

It was a short game, but Adam and I won. We didn't win anything except for bragging rights, but that was enough for me. It got my mind off the whole Grunt situation, which made me feel a lot better. It's nice to hang out with friends who actually have a good time with me. I wonder what sort of cool thing I'll get up to tomorrow.

Day Twenty-Two: Am I a Wizard?

Dear Diary,

    I didn't have any plans today because Snow had plans and I still was mad at Grunt for being mad at me for no good reason. Next week is going to be the last week of science class, so I decided to get some studying done.

    Usually, studying would have been boring, but I discovered something that really caught my interest. When I was looking through my chemistry book I noticed that the experiment that I did a really good job on the other day matched up perfectly to a potion in another book that my mom had. That could only mean one thing. I had made a potion.

I thought that only witches could make potions, but I was a guy and a zombie. Did that mean that I was a wizard zombie? I had no idea what any of this meant, but I knew that I wanted to look into it more. I spent the whole day studying to find out, and it didn't feel like studying at all. It was actually kind of fun.

Even though I studied all day, I still didn't know if I was a wizard or not, or if it was even possible for me to be one. I didn't want to ask my mom about it because it sounded silly in my head, so I bet it would sound even sillier if I said it out loud. Besides, my mom might not even know. There was only one person who would know if I was a wizard for not: Miss Enchantment.

I'm going to ask Miss Enchantment if I'm a wizard after class tomorrow. She's the only one who can tell me what I really am. I don't even know if I'll be able to sleep or not tonight. I'm too excited to find out if I'm magic or not!

Day Twenty-Three: Who Can be Magic?

Dear Diary,

Today would have been one of those days that I can't pay attention in class, but even though I was distracted by the idea that I might be a wizard, the only way that I could find more clues to figure out if I was magical was to pay attention in class.

When class was over I had finally learned something without getting distracted and I was ready to ask Miss

Enchantment my question. I stayed behind after class until all of the kids had left. When Miss Enchantment saw me waiting around she said, "You did a really good job last week on your experiment, you don't need to stay for tutoring anymore."

For a minute I forgot that I usually came for tutoring around this time every week. "I know that I don't have tutoring today. I wanted to talk to you about something else."

Miss Enchantment looked confused. "What's up?"

I told her all about the studying that I did and how I found out that the experiment that we did last week was the same thing as a potion. Miss Enchantment looked a little impressed to see that I had found this out. Finally, I got to what I had really been waiting to ask. "Since I made a potion, does that mean that I'm magic?"

For a second I thought that Miss Enchantment was going to laugh at me, but I was glad that she didn't. "Only witches can be magic, but that doesn't mean that you can't make potions." She went on to explain that anyone who was smart enough could make a potion, but only witches could actually do magic. I was a little confused by this, but my main question was answered. I wasn't a wizard, but I was a really smart zombie, and that was still pretty to hear. It was actually nice to hear Miss Enchantment say that I'm smart. I'll be sure to use more of my smarts in class tomorrow, too.

Day Twenty-Four: Bad News and Worries

Dear Diary,

The second time that I pay full attention in class and I get bad news. I'm starting to think that paying attention in class just isn't right for me. I don't even want to write down this bad news, but I know that I have to. On Friday class will be over, which is pretty good. On Friday we won't be ending the class with a big party like what Ms. Skele did in our history class. Instead, our class is going to end with a...final exam.

A final exam really is as bad as it sounds. It's basically a test that covers everything that we've learned this month. That's not even the worst part! This test counts for half of our whole grade. If someone fails this test, then they'll probably fail the class. I write "they" because I'm not really worried about myself. I've been studying a lot and I still have a few days to study some more, so I'm sure that I'll pass this test.

Even though I'm not worried about my own grades, I'm still really worried about Grunt's grades. I haven't talked to him since the last time I tried to convince him to go to a tutoring lesson. Even though he's mad at me, I think I need to try to convince him to study again. If he fails this test then he' going to fail summer school and he'll be stuck in elementary school for another year.

I'm not even sure that Grunt will want my help, but I know that he needs it. I'm determined to help him to study, even if he tries to ignore me again. Maybe saving his grades will be the thing that makes him stop being mad at me. Of course, bugging him about it could be the thing that ends our friendship... I think it's worth the risk! I'm going to talk to Grunt about this if it's the last thing I do! But...I think I'm going to do it tomorrow. I'll write all about it then.

Day Twenty-Five: Scheduling a Study Session

Dear Diary,

I thought about making a plan to get Grunt to study, but last time I had a plan and it didn't work at all. I wasn't about to waste a whole day trying to make another plan, so I decided that I was just going to wing it. Besides, my plan can't fail if I don't have one, to begin with.

When class was over I ran up to Grunt. I thought about tackling him to get his attention, but yelling his name seemed to do the trick. "What do you want?" Grunt mumbled at me. "I don't want to talk to you about anything."

"That's fine. I don't need you to talk. I need you to study." I made sure to sound like a strict parent so that he would have to listen to me.

"I'm not going to that tutoring thing. There's no way that I'm going to spend any extra time with Miss Enchantment if I don't have to." He sounded angry and by this time he was already out of the school and heading towards his mom's car.

"I know you don't want my help, but you need it!" I yelled when I got to the car, and Grunt's mom heard me.

"What does he need your help with?" She asked me.

Grunt looked at me like he didn't want me to say anything, but that's how I knew that I had to say something. I looked right at Grunt's mom and told her, "Grunt's failing this science class, and if he doesn't get his act together he's going to fail summer school."

Both Grunt and his mom looked really mad when I said this. Apparently, Grunt's mom didn't know that Grunt was failing, and she wasn't happy to hear about it. She looked at Grunt and said, "You're studying with him tomorrow whether you like it or not." Grunt looked really mad at me when he got into his mom's car.

I knew it wasn't cool of me to tell his mom his secret, but I knew it was the right thing to do. We will study together tomorrow. Even if he ends up hating me for this, I know that with my help he can pass this class, and that is what's really important to me.

Day Twenty-Six: Frenemies no More

Dear Diary,

Grunt's mom drove me home with them after school today. I was nervous in the car because Grunt was still really mad at me. I was worried that he was going to punch me or something while his mom wasn't looking. Luckily, he didn't try anything mean, but that didn't make me any less nervous.

When we got to his house we went to his room to start studying. I hadn't been to his house in weeks because he had been mad at me, but it looked just liked I remembered. I set out some of the chemistry books on his desk and started reading my notes to him so that he could copy them down to study later.

After we studied for an hour Grunt's mom knocked on the door and said that we could be done if we wanted. She offered me some snacks and I took them. I was about to leave when something strange happened: Grunt asked me if I wanted to stay for a little longer and play video games with him. I pleasantly surprised by this, and I agreed to stay.

Two hours later, and five finished video games levels beat, Grunt and I were talking like best friends again. It was like we had never gotten into a fight in the first place. It wasn't just like we were best friends again, we were best friends again.

When I was about to leave, Grunt told me, "I'm sorry that I was being such a jerk earlier. I just hate it when I feel stupid, and that happens whenever you turn out to be smart in class. I know it's not your fault, but it still makes me mad. I'm going to study really hard tonight so that I can be prepared for that test. Thanks for helping me out so much."

I was glad to hear Grunt say this. It felt nice to finally hear an apology. "No problem," I told him. I was smiling now. It was the first time that I smiled while thinking about Grunt in a long time. It was nice to have my best friend back. I bet tomorrow is going to be even better because of it.

Day Twenty-Seven: Test Day

Dear Diary,

After leaving Grunt's house yesterday I went back home and studied some more. The test was today and I wanted to be as prepared as I could be. This test counted for a big part of my grade and I wanted to do a good job on it. My head was so full of science facts that by the end of the night I thought my head was going to explode like a Creeper who gets scared.

When it was finally time for the test

I was ready for it. I looked over to Grunt before the test began to give him a thumb's up. He gave me one back, so I knew that he was ready for this test. Miss Enchantment told us to clear our desks (except for a pencil) and handed out the tests. It took me about twenty minutes to finish, and the whole class was done within half an hour. It really wasn't as hard as I thought it would be.

When everyone was done Miss Enchantment took back the tests and handed out something out: pieces of cake! She had planned a party to celebrate the end of class but she didn't tell any of us because she wanted it to be a surprise. Let me write this: it worked!

We ate cake, played music, and had a great time. It was the perfect way to end the class. Now I just hope that my grades will be perfect enough for me to pass the test...

Day Twenty-Eight: The Best of Friends

Dear Diary,

Since class was over and Grunt and I were friends again, we decided to hang out. I already had made plans with Snow for this weekend because I didn't actually think that I would be friends with Grunt again by now. I was glad that we were friends again, but it did complicate my plans. Luckily, Snow is flexible with her plans, even if she doesn't have any muscles to be flexible with. She agreed to let Grunt join us, and I was glad that she did. We had a great time together.

We all hung out at this park next to Snow's house. She lives in a mainly Skeleton village so the whole park was themed to look like bones. It was kind of spooky, but really cool at the same time. They have this giant fake skull on the playground that everyone plays a game called "king of the skull" on. I never heard of the game, so Snow taught me and Grunt how to play.

Basically, the first person to stand on the top of the fake skull for a minute straight would win. This was a lot harder than it sounded. It took like twenty minutes for one of us to do this. It was no surprise that Snow won the game. First of all, she knew how to play before us, but the thing that really helped her to win is that Skeletons are a lot faster than Zombies.

Even though Grunt and I lost, Snow still gave us some snacks for being good sports. When we were done with our snacks Grunt and I went home. When I got home I remembered that I have something to look forward to tomorrow. My grades are coming in, and I'll find out if I passed this science class or not. I'm feeling pretty good about it. I'm just a little worried about Grunt's grades. I hope that he passes this class. I guess he and I will both find out our fates tomorrow.

Day Twenty-Nine: Passing Party

Dear Diary,

This morning I got a two letters in the mail today. Well, they were addressed to "The Parents of Ugh," but I knew that meant that they were really for me. I tore open the first letter and saw my grade for the science class I just finished...I got a B+! I passed the class, and with a really good grade, too! I ran into my parent's room and showed them the letter. They looked so proud to see my grade.

They called up Grunt and Snow's

parents to invite everyone over for a party while I put the second letter in my room to open later. I didn't know what this one said, and I wanted to open it in private in case it was full of something that my parents would be upset about, like a letter from Miss Enchantment telling them that I hardly ever paid attention in class or something.

Eventually, my friends and their parents showed up to my place and we ate some pizza together and had a good time. I was distracted from all of this until I got a chance to talk to Grunt. I still didn't know if he passed the class at this point, and I needed to talk to him. "How'd you do?" I asked him.

"I got a D." It was a low grade, but it was a passing grade! I gave Grunt a high-five and we went back to the party.

I was so glad to hear that Grunt was going onto the third part of summer school with me. He was almost done...that meant that I was almost done. I have one more class to do, and then I'm done with summer school, which means that I'll make it into middle school. I can't wait!

Day Thirty: What's Next?

Dear Diary,

Today I remembered all about the second letter that I got in the mail yesterday. With the party and everything going on yesterday I totally forgot about the letter. I still wanted to open it in private in case it was a bad letter, so I opened it in my room before I even changed out of my pajamas.

I opened the letter slowly so that it wouldn't make a lot of noise. I took the letter out of the envelope. I read the letter carefully and found out that there wasn't really much for me to worry about. All the letter said was that I was moving on to my next summer school class...which happened to be a gym class that was taught by a Blaze.

I had never really showed up to a gym class before, which was probably why I had to take a gym class this summer. I had totally forgotten about needing to retake a gym class...mostly because I had forgotten that I even taken a gym class. I guess I'm going to need to work out instead of study if I want to do well in this class.

Well, now I know what next month has in store for me. I just hope that I can keep up with the rest of the monsters in the class, literally. I guess I'll find out if I have what takes next month. I'll be sure to write all about it in my diary next month. Until then, I've got a day full of partying to do before I go back to school!

Book 3: My Gym Teacher is a Blaze

Day One: Passing Classes

Dear Diary,

My name is Ugh, and I'm finally going into my last class for the summer, which means that this will be my last diary. My mom made me keep a diary over the summer as a punishment for failing three classes during the school year. Personally, I thought that summer school was punishment enough, but my mom didn't agree. Writing these diaries actually hasn't been half bad, though. I'm kind of glad that my mom made me do this--not that I'm going to tell her that.

In the first diary that she made me write, I wrote all about how crazy it was to have a Skeleton as a history teacher. Her name was Ms. Skele, and she was actually pretty cool. She was super old, like older than the oldest great-great grandmas out there. She fought in an extreme war and did other cool things during her lifetime. She told us all about it, which helped to make the class really interesting. I wrote all about what she taught us in my first diary, so I won't write about it all day in this one.

In my second diary, I wrote all about a science class that I had with a woman who was half human-half witch named Miss Enchantment. We did some experiments...which I wasn't so good at in the beginning, but I eventually got the hang of it. I even made a potion once! It was pretty cool. Of course, I wrote all about it in my second diary, and I want to leave as much room as possible in this diary for all of the cool stuff that I'm going to get up to this month.

My gym class starts on Monday, and I'm sure it's going to be wild. I mean, it kind of has to be, especially since it's being taught by one of the most hardcore Blazes in the area. I heard he was sent here straight from the Nether... I just hope that I can take the heat this month!

Day Two: Friends in Different Places

Dear Diary,

My two best friends in the world are Grunt and Snow. I've known Grunt for pretty much my entire life. We actually did a pretty good job of helping each other get into summer school. We used to skip classes all of the time together, and it turns out that when you skip class a lot you kind of don't learn much... Grunt and I have our ups and downs, but we always end up being best friends in the end.

I only met Snow in my history class this summer. She had transferred to my school in the middle of the school year, so she had trouble keeping up in class. She's a lot different than Grunt. We never really have any fights or anything like that. She's just a really nice girl, actually. I know that I can always count on her.

The one flaw with my best friends is that they are great at gym class, meaning that they actually showed up to gym class. Instead of suffering in gym class with me this summer Grunt is going to be taking an English class and Snow is taking a math class. I did pretty well in those classes during the school year, so I don't need to redo those ones. I just really hate gym class, so I never showed up. It's just that zombies are a lot slower than most monsters, which means that we tend to get picked on the most. Now I'm going to have to show up to gym class every weekday this month if I want to pass the class.

My first gym class starts tomorrow at dusk. I hope that the kids in the summer gym class are nicer than the ones who are in the class during the school year. I guess the kids who failed gym class during the school year must feel the same way about gym class as I do, so maybe we'll get along. I guess I'll just have to wait until tomorrow to find out. I'll write all about it tomorrow.

Day Three: The First Day of Gym

Dear Diary,

"Is it hot in here or is it just me?" I said as I walked into the gym today. I thought it was a little bit of a funny joke, but Mr. Inferno didn't agree.

"Actually, I think it's just me." He said in reply to my joke.

I had never seen a real life Blaze until today. I live in the Overworld, and most Blazes tend to live in the Nether. I had seen some in pictures before, but it was totally different to see one floating right next to me. I don't know what made him qualified to teach a gym class, but if I had to guess I would say that it was probably his ability to scare kids into exercising. It wasn't that Mr. Inferno actually looked like a mean guy, but he sure did look like a scary guy. He was literally a ball of floating fire with eyes. I had no idea how he wasn't setting the whole building on fire by just being there. For his sake and mine, I really hoped that most of the classes would be held outside.

"Line up!" Mr. Inferno yelled to the class. None of us wanted to try to argue him, so we all got in a straight line up against one of the walls of the gym. Mr. Inferno took attendance for the class and then he had something else to say, "There are a few rules here, so I need you to listen up."

"There will be no talking while I'm talking, it's just disrespectful. No one will be mean to anyone else. We don't need that kind of drama here. Basically, just be nice, listen to me, and don't fool around. Got it?"

The whole class nodded or said something along the lines of "yes" in agreement.

The rest of the class period was spent in a sort of free day. I shot some basketballs by myself because I didn't know anyone else in the class. There was a big mix of grades here, so I didn't really know who I would play with anyway. Mr. Inferno says that he has something planned for tomorrow, so I guess that I can look forward to that. I'll write all about what happens tomorrow.

Day Four: The Challenge

Dear Diary,

Since the whole class just went through introductions and rules yesterday, today was pretty much the first real day of gym class, and Mr. Inferno let us know it. Today we weren't going to have another free day or even play any sports. Today we were just being challenged to the extremes of fitness.

Mr. Inferno made all of the kids line up against the wall again so that he could take attendance. Everyone was here, which

I was a little surprised by. This was the slacker class, and I knew it. These kids' parents must have really been pushing them to succeed, and that's what Mr. Inferno was doing too.

The first challenge of the day was push-ups. I didn't do a very good job. I was only able to do fifteen in one minute. One kid in the class, Bruiser (that's his real name), managed to do sixty in one minute! That's one a second! The next challenge was pull-ups, which is way harder than a push-up. I couldn't even do one, but I didn't feel super bad because most kids couldn't do any either.

After pull-ups was running. I don't know how slow I was, all I knew is that I lapped the first time when someone finished their third lap. By the time I finished all three laps, there were only five minutes left in class. Everyone else was already packing up their stuff and getting ready to leave.

As I left, I saw Mr. Inferno put up

the score for all of the challenges. I looked for my name to find out how well I did, but I found it in the same spot every time--dead last. I wonder if this whole thing will ruin my grade or not. I really hope not. I would hate to be held back just because of a gym class.

I hope that tomorrow goes a lot better than today. My legs hurt from all of the running, and I'm not sure that I could take another day like this one...

Day Five: Dodgeball

Dear Diary,

When Mr. Inferno announced that we would be playing dodgeball today I thought to myself, "Ah yes, this is my time to shine!" Dodgeball was basically the lazy zombie's sport, and if I was anything I was definitely a lazy zombie. All I had to do was avoid getting hit by a ball and throw a few back. At least, that's how dodgeball works in my head...it didn't actually play out like that in real life.

Mr. Inferno wanted the teams to be

fair, so he picked them himself. He didn't want friends to group up or have anyone not get picked for a team. I was on the red team. We had to wear these old jerseys that were in the storage room. They smelled really bad, and that's coming from a zombie that literally smells like death.

I got on my side of the gym and grabbed a ball as soon as the game started. I threw it to the other side as hard as I could. I was sure that the ball was going to plant some kid right in the face. It did hit a kid...in the hands...meaning that he caught it and I was out. I spent the rest of the first game out.

The rest of the games went a lot like the first one. One time I accidentally threw a ball at one of the girls on my own team. The rest of my team didn't like that too much... I swear that I was out of the games longer than I was in most of them. I think I even made more enemies than friends while I was playing too.

All in all, today was pretty much just the worst. I hope that things start to get more fun in this class. If it doesn't, then I'll just be tempted to skip classes again, and I know that I can't do that. I just hope that I can be determined enough to keep coming to class.

Day Six: Picked Last

Dear Diary,

Today we were going to play dodgeball again, and as soon as Mr. Inferno mentioned this I wanted to skip class. It took everything I had and knowing that my mom was knitting in the parking lot, to make me stay in class I know I cannot skip class.

The game was a little different today because Mr. Inferno didn't pick the teams. He figured that we were able to show our class what we were good at, so instead, he just picked two team captains that picked the teams. I wasn't on the red team today, which was nice. The only reason that I wasn't on the red team is that they got to pick first, so I just ended up on the other team because I was picked last.

My team really hated me because I was bad at the game. I got out only half as much as I did the last time I played, but my team didn't seem to care much about that. They only thing they cared about was that I was really bad at the game last time. They were hardly even giving me a chance to improve before they started judging me.

By the end of the game, everyone still felt like I wasn't any good at sports. At least tomorrow is Friday so that I can have a little bit of a break after class tomorrow. I just need a day without exercise. I need a day to relax...

Day Seven: Kids Like Me

Dear Diary,

When I first saw Mr. Inferno I thought he was going to be super scary and angry all of the time, but I've learned that just because a guy is literally made out of fire doesn't mean that he's got a hot temper. He even let us have a free day today because it's Friday. He also said something about every Friday being a free day so long as everyone behaves well during the rest of the school week. This is basically just like having a recess for an hour. I think that I can get used to this.

What I can't get used to is playing alone. Sure, shooting hoops by myself isn't that bad, but I knew that I would have a lot more fun if I had someone to play with me. I wish that I could have convinced Grunt to skip more gym classes with me during the school year so that he would be stuck here with me now. I guess I could have gone to more gym classes during the school year to avoid this too...oh well.

I had to make some new friends, that was the only solution. I just had to figure out what kinds of kids I wanted to be friends with. I knew that I couldn't directly go to the kids who were awesome at sports. They didn't want to have anything to do with me. I had to aim for the kids who were bad at sports like me, and I knew just who to talk to.

There was another zombie in the class who was just as slow as I was. His name was Gene. There was a Skeleton who had no hand-eye coordination at all named Tibby. She wasn't much help on the gym floor, but she was really nice to talk to. We decided to hang out together since no one else really wanted to play with us.

None of us were really good at sports, so we played a game that we made up called "roll the ball." We sat on the floor in a triangle and rolled a ball back and forth with each other and just talked about stuff. It was really nice to meet some kids that didn't just care about my sports skills. I might even hang out with these guys outside of class sometimes since they're so cool.

Today was a really good day. I hope that there're more days like this in this class. It would really make me feel better about the whole thing. I think this class is going to get better and better if I keep making great friends like Tibby and Gene.

Day Eight: Snow and Grunt

Dear Diary,

I'm so tired from working out every day that I was glad to finally have a day off just to hang out with my friends. I was really curious to find out what they have been doing in their classes. I imagined that hearing about them sitting in desks all day would be able to help me to feel like I had just been sitting on my butt all week instead of being hit with dodgeballs.

I asked Grunt about his English class, and he actually was acting pretty thrilled about it. I was a little jealous that I wasn't in his class. It sounded pretty fun. I guess it was because Ms. Skele was teaching the English class too, so a lot of the kids were writing stories about whatever they wanted. I guess they were also reading some really cool books. It sounded a lot better than the gym class that I was in. I asked Grunt if he wanted to trade classes with me since he loved gym and his English class sounded really cool, but he only laughed instead of actually answering me. I guess that's just what happens when you're so funny that people don't know when you're joking and when you're not.

Snow's math class is just being taught by our normal math teacher, and it doesn't sound very exciting. Then again, when is a math class ever exciting? She did tell us a pretty funny story about something that happened during class. I guess that one day the teacher just didn't show up because he was sick or something, so one of the kids just pretended to teach the class for the whole day, she even assigned pretend homework. The best part of the story is that the next day everyone actually did that homework, which was the first time that everyone turned in their homework.

Tomorrow I'm going to spend the day with Roarbert. He said that he wanted to do something with me, which came as a surprise to me. I guess I'll just have to wait until tomorrow to find out what he has planned.

Day Nine: Roarbert's Secret

Dear Diary,

Roarbert told me something strange today. It's totally changed how I'm going to think about him from now on. I've been telling Roarbert about my gym class all week. I told him that I was no good at it and that the other kids were making fun of me for it. Usually, Roarbert would have laughed right with the mean kids, but this time, he wanted to help. That's when he told me his secret.

"I've never told anyone this before,

but I'm actually really good at sports. I'm not even just good for a zombie, I'm just as good as a human who is good at sports."

I couldn't believe what he was saying at first. No zombie could be that good at sports. Besides, I had never seen Roarbert throw or catch a ball in his life, so how could he be good at sports? "Prove it," I told him. I must have sounded a lot tougher than I thought I did because he took me up on the challenge.

We went out into our backyard and Roarbert pulled out a baseball and a bat. I didn't even know that we had this stuff. He must have been hiding it, but I don't know why he would want to hide it in the first place. I guess that he really did want to keep his sports skills a secret.

"Throw the ball to me as hard as you can," Roarbert said. He raised bat up high, ready to hit the ball.

I threw the ball as hard as I could. It wasn't a very good throw, but Roarbert was able to hit it way out of the backyard. I had no choice but to believe that he was great at sports.

For the rest of the night, Roarbert taught me everything that he knew about sports so that I would be able to do a better job in my gym class. I guess that I'll get to test my sweet skills out tomorrow. I just hope I can remember everything that I learned tonight.

Day Ten: Lost and on a Run

Dear Diary,

Today Mr. Inferno announced that we were going to do one of the only things that are worse than getting hit in the face with a dodgeball. We had to run. That wasn't even the worst part of it. We had to run a whole mile, outside, in the dark. To be fair, Zombies pretty much did everything in the dark, but running in the dark was pretty new to me.

Mr. Inferno gave each of us a light to use to guide our way on the path that he marked off. He told us just to follow the path and we would be fine. The winners would get a prize. The losers would just be ashamed of themselves. Those are Mr.Inferno's words, not mine. Mr. Inferno was also being really lazy. He set us up to run, but he wasn't going to run with us. He was just going to wait at the starting line, which also happened to be the finish line.

I started to run with my new group of friends, and I was doing pretty well in the beginning because it was all downhill. I even eventually caught up with one of the most athletic kids in the class. That's when the trouble started. "Want to take a short cut?" Usually, I wouldn't cheat, but I really hated running, so I agreed. The only problem was that this kid was way faster than me as he ran through the woods, and it wasn't marked, which is how I got lost.

I stopped running once I realized that I was lost. I had to find my way out, but everywhere I looked I could only see trees. I started walking back to where I entered the woods and found something that was alive...a Creeper! I started backing away slowly so that I wouldn't freak it out, but I accidentally stepped on a stick that makes a loud cracking sound and the Creeper started to flip out. Seconds later, the thing had exploded. I wasn't hurt, though. The explosion did make a clearing in the woods, too, so I was able to find my way out safely.

I left the woods and got back on track. Sure, I was the last one to cross the finish line, but it was better than being the first one to get blown up by a Creeper. Mr. Inferno was mad that I was so late, but I didn't actually get in trouble.

I don't know what we're doing tomorrow, but I'm sure that I'll be better than this. I need to rest...

Day Eleven: High Praise

Dear Diary,

The weather was still nice today, so Mr. Inferno just lets everyone play outside on the playground for gym class today. The playground is probably one of the only things that I'll miss when I'm out of elementary school; the middle school doesn't have one. I knew that I had to enjoy it while I could.

I was chilling on the swings when a kid decided to swing with me. I had seen the kid around our class before, but I couldn't remember his name. Apparently, he remembered mine. "Hey Ugh, I heard a big explosion in the woods the other day when you were taking the short cut. What happened?"

I was a little embarrassed that he heard the Creeper explode, but no one else was around, so I told him everything that had happened yesterday. It turned out that there was no real reason to feel embarrassed anyway, this kid thought it was super cool that I scared the Creeper, even if I didn't mean to do it.

By the end of the gym class, nearly everyone had heard the story of how I defeated the Creeper. At least, that's how the story had changed in the hour. I wasn't about to correct them, though. If they thought I was cool, then I was going to let them keep thinking just that...as long as Mr. Inferno didn't hear about it, then I'll spill my guts and tell him the real story so I don't get in trouble.

Now that a lot of the kids think I'm

cool, I think this class is going to be a lot easier for me. I can just feel it.

Tomorrow's going to be a great day. I'm almost excited for my gym class now. I'll write all about it tomorrow!

Day Twelve: Baseball

Dear Diary,

I was starting to wonder when I would get to try out those baseball skills that I learned from Roarbert, and today was finally the day!

Mr. Inferno had set up a baseball diamond outside of the school for us to use today. He picked the teams again, and from there the kids got to pick who did what. When I wasn't hitting the balls, I would be the pitcher. It was hard to convince my team to let me do this, but since my popularity upgrade yesterday, the kids let me have a chance to prove myself.

My goal was to throw the ball at a weird angle so that it would be hard to hit. I also wanted to throw it slowly so that if someone on the other team did hit it, they wouldn't be able to hit it very far. At least, that's how I think baseball must work.

I got up to pitch...and I didn't do especially well at first. A couple kids even got on the bases, so my team wasn't so happy with me. I had to be serious about this. I did my best to strike out the next three people...and I didn't. I did strike out three out of four of the next four, though. The other team only got one point, which wasn't too bad.

My team was pretty good at batting, and I even got to make a home run. It was pretty fun. The rest of the game went along pretty well, and in the end, my team won by two points. Since I didn't totally stink at this game, the kids liked me even more than usual. I think if I can keep this up then my popularity will soar. I'll be the coolest kid in school. I can't wait!

Day Thirteen: Fencing, AKA Sword Fighting

Dear Diary,

I think I found my new favorite sport. I didn't even know it was a sport until today, but I'm glad that Mr. Inferno knew about it. Today we had fencing lessons. The word "fencing" kind of makes it sound like we were going to be painting fences all day, but instead fencing is basically learning how to sword fight, and I am all up for that.

Everyone got a dull sword so that

no one would actually get hurt. We were put into pairs to practice. I was practicing with this kid named Party, but I don't think that was his name. I just heard that his birthday parties are always really cool. Even if his parties were cool, his sword fighting skills weren't. If we would have had real swords, his leg would have been cut off, but since it was fake he just pretended it was cut off and he jumped on one foot for the rest of the match. It was fun. Oh, and I won.

I think that I'm actually pretty good at this sport. I wonder if I can get Roarbert or one of my other friends to do this with me. Maybe I can teach my big brother about a new sport. That would be kind of cool. Well, tomorrow is Friday, so I'm sure that I'll have a good time in class. After that, the weekend is all mine to do with what I want. I might sword fight my brother, my friends, or anyone who gets in my way. I'm just kidding about that last one, though. No matter what happens, I'm sure that I'll have a great weekend.

Day Fourteen: Friday Free Day

Dear Diary,

Today was another free day, but it went a lot better than the last free day that we had. I didn't need to sit around playing roll the ball with the other kids who weren't good at sports. I was invited to play whatever sport I wanted, even with the cool kids in the class. Of course, I wasn't just going to ignore Tibby and the rest of the kids who are bad at sports just because I'm okay at sports now. It just wouldn't be cool of me.

Instead of just hanging out with one group of kids, I decided to take turns playing with pretty much everyone in the class. I guess that I'm getting pretty popular around the gym. I decided to do my new favorite thing with my old friends and my new ones: sword fight. I got out a couple of wooden swords and challenged anyone I could to a fight.

The rules were simple: if you get hit in an arm or leg, you have to pretend like it got cut off. If you get hit in the head or the body you've got to pretend that you're dead and the game's over. I challenged just about every kid in the class. I would like to say that I won every match, but that's not true. I did win most of the matches that I was in, which was pretty cool.

I was right about today being good. Since tomorrow is Saturday, I bet things will be even better. I have plans to hang out with Grunt, so I'm sure that hanging out with him will be fun. I can't wait until I see him!

Day Fifteen: Fencing with Roarbert and Grunt

Dear Diary,

Even though I had the day off from school, I still wanted to do some stuff that I learned in my gym class. So far my favorite thing that I learned in class was fencing, and I wanted to show off my new skills to my friend and my brother. After all, Roarbert had taught me how to play baseball. I figured it would be cool to teach him how to do this.

I invited Grunt to come over today

so that I could teach him and Roarbert how to play the game at the same time. Plus, I figured that it would be extra fun if there were three people against each other instead of just two. Mr. Inferno had even let me borrow some wooden swords to use over the weekend because I mentioned that I wanted to practice.

I showed Roarbert the swords first and told him all about what I learned in school. He thought it was pretty cool. I showed him a few of my moves before Grunt showed up. To prank him. Roarbert and I hid behind some trees near our house. When we saw Grunt coming, we snuck up behind him and spooked him. He freaked out, so I threw him the last sword and challenged him to a fight as soon as he realized we were just pranking him.

The game went just as great as I thought it would go. By the end of the day, Grunt and Roarbert were almost as good as I was. Eventually, we got tired of playing with the swords and we just sat around and played video games and ate some snacks instead, but we still had a really good day.

I'm going to hang out with Snow tomorrow. She called earlier and said that she had a surprise set up for me, and I'm a little nervous and excited to see what it is. I hope it'll be as fun as what we did today!

Day Sixteen: Snow's Surprise

Dear Diary,

    I walked over to Snow's house today to find out what her surprise was all about. I had no idea what it was going to be, which I guess made it a really good surprise. Snow asked me to meet her in her backyard. When I got there I saw that there were a bunch of targets set up.

    "I called you yesterday to plan something for today, but your brother picked up and said that you had been practicing sword fighting all day. I figured since you liked that so much you might like to try to shoot some arrows with me. Skeletons are usually pretty good at it, so I have some extra bows and arrows lying around the house that my mom said we could use."

I was pretty impressed to see that Snow had set up all this just since she called my house yesterday. It was a really nice thing of her to do. Of course, I had never actually shot an arrow before, so I didn't know if it was going to go well or not...and it didn't.

As it turns out, sword fighting and shooting arrows are nothing alike. I might be the best sword fighter in my gym class, but I think I might be the worst arrow shooter in the world. Snow tried her best to teach me, but I couldn't hit even a single target. I think I might have accidentally shot down a bat once...but I don't think that counts for anything. Snow was shooting a target every time she tried to--she even got a few bull eyes. It was pretty impressive.

When we were done doing this, Snow offered to give me more lessons so that I could get better, but I turned her down. I'd rather spend my time doing something that I know that I can stand a chance at, like the cake eating contest she and I had after our practice.

Anyway, I'm all rested and ready for whatever my gym class has to throw at me tomorrow. I just hope something fun is thrown at me instead of a dodgeball.

Day Seventeen: Tests? Again?

Dear Diary,

Today I returned the wooden swords to Mr. Inferno, and I expected him to say thanks, but instead he just made me line up for attendance like the rest of the kids. Then he said something really mean to me, and to the rest of the class, "Today we're going to be doing some testing again."

I could hardly believe that we had to do this junk again. I thought the testing was a one-time thing, but Mr. Inferno made it clear today that we would be doing this sort of thing every Monday until the class was over. He also mentioned that we were going to be graded on this, which kind of stressed me out until he mentioned that we just had to do better than we did last time.

I did my best, which still wasn't very good... I did pretty much the same on most of the stuff, which made me pretty nervous. I want to do well in this class so that I can move onto middle school. I would hate to be held back just because I failed a gym class. I did do better on two parts of the test, though. I wasn't last in the race this time, which was really cool, actually. I also managed to do one pull-up. Some kids still couldn't do any! I bet it was all the sword fighting I did over the week. It must have made my arm muscles strong.

Once we were done with our tests, Mr. Inferno let us go home early. I was glad. I really needed to rest. He also said that we're going to do something fun tomorrow, so I'm looking forward to that. Really, I'm looking forward to anything that isn't another test...

Day Eighteen: Volleyball

Dear Diary,

Today we actually got to do something fun in gym class. We were playing a game called volleyball. I had heard of it before, but I had never actually played it before today. We were going to play it outside, but it was raining today so we had to play it in the gym.

I was on a team with Tibby and another kid who I had been getting along with named Will. I didn't know how it was going to go, but I was still excited to play.

I was glad that I wasn't first up to hit the ball because I wasn't really sure how to do it. Tibby was up first so I got to watch how she did it. She threw the ball up in the air, and as it fell down she hit it so hard that it flew over to the other team's side of the court, which I guess what's supposed to happen. What I didn't expect was for the ball to get hit back over to our side and come directly at me!

I did swing my arms in front of me, and accidentally hit the ball, but it did land on the other side and didn't come back. I had scored a point! As the teams kept taking turns I got braver when the ball came at me. By the end of the game, I wasn't flinching anymore. Of course, that doesn't necessarily mean that I was any good at the sport. I actually proved that I was pretty bad at it when it was my turn to hit the ball first. I threw it in the air just like Tibby did. I hit it on the way down, but I didn't hit it all the way to the other side. It hit Will right on the top of the head. I don't think I need to write it for it to be obvious, but my team didn't get a point for that throw.

My team actually lost the game, which made me feel pretty bad. I hope that kids don't start being mean to me again because I helped our team to lose. I guess I'll just need to wait until tomorrow to find out.

Day Nineteen: Confused, but Happy

Dear Diary,

Today I was kind of bummed out to hear that we would be playing volleyball again. The last thing I wanted was to be picked last and to not be popular again. All the kids in this class seemed to care about was how good someone was at sports. I was worried that they wouldn't like me anymore because I stunk yesterday.

I was really confused, but happy, to find out that the kids thought that I was still cool even thought I lost the game yesterday. I didn't even get picked last this time! I was pretty happy to see that these kids didn't just care about me for my sports skills, which I had very little of.

I still didn't do very well today, but I did manage to make a new friend today. His name was Sky and he wasn't very good at volleyball either, so at least we had that in common. We actually stunk at the game more than we did yesterday because we were talking through the whole game.

We may have lost the game again, but I think that I made a friend, which is way better than winning the game, anyway.

I hope that we do something new tomorrow, but even if we don't I won't be upset. I feel like I'm making a new friend every day. Maybe this gym class isn't so bad after all. I can't wait until tomorrow!

Day Twenty: Sky

Dear Diary,

Today we just played volleyball again, so I'm not going to waste my diary entry writing about the same old thing every day. I do have something a little more exciting to write about, though. After school, Sky came home with me to hang out because we were getting along so well while we were losing volleyball games together.

I brought Sky home and introduced him to Roarbert and my parents. He ate dinner with my family and he really got along with everyone, even Roarbert which I hardly would have imagined that anyone would be able to get along with Roarbert as soon as they met him.

I got to know Sky a little better today, too. I guess he didn't fail gym because he didn't show up, he just failed because he didn't do a very good job at it. If he wasn't my friend, I probably would have made fun of him for it, but since we were I decided not to say anything rude. Besides, if I made fun of him for that he would be able to tease me for skipping school.

I also found out that he was really good at drawing. He drew a picture of me and it looked almost exactly like me. I mean, it probably wasn't all that hard because I'm a pretty square guy. I'm not very good at drawing, so I just challenged him to some video games and a snack eating contest (I won) once he was done drawing.

I would say that we had a pretty good time today, and I bet that we're going to keep hanging out at school tomorrow. After all, tomorrow is Friday, so I'm sure that the free day is going to be even better than it usually is now that I have so many friends. I'll write all about it tomorrow.

Day Twenty-One: Beach Free Day

Dear Diary,

Today there was a path of minecarts parked in front of the school. I had no idea what it was for, but Mr. Inferno did. He had all of us line up like every day to take attendance and then he said, "I have good news and bad news. The bad news is that today's class will be twice as long as usual," The whole class groaned at this. Mr. Inferno continued on. "The good news is that we won't be going to the gym today...we're going to the beach!" Instead of groaning, the class cheered.

Since I had been in summer school almost literally all summer I hadn't had time to go to the beach, so I was really pumped to be able to go during class since I probably wouldn't have time to go after class.

The whole class and Mr. Inferno hopped into a minecart as it drove us to the beach. The moon was out and it was shining brightly. The water looked black because of the night sky. It looked really cool. I ran into the water as soon as I could and my friends followed quickly behind me. The water was cold, but it felt pretty good.

Even though we spent twice the normal amount of time at the beach, it felt like half the normal time because I was having so much fun. My friends and I played a couple games of chicken, tossed around a beach ball, and had a pretty big splash fight. I almost wish that gym class had lasted even longer today.

Well, tomorrow is Saturday, so I'm

sure that I'll be able to fill my day with even more fun stuff. I've got to remember to hang out with Grunt and Snow this weekend. I've been missing them now that I don't have a class with them anymore. I'll write all about whatever we do tomorrow.

Day Twenty-Two: The Friends of my Friends are my Friends

Dear Diary,

Today I invited Tibby to hang out with me. I wanted her to meet Snow and Grunt. I figured that she would get along really well with my other friends, especially Snow since they were both girl Skeletons. I told everyone to meet up at the beach since I had such a fun time there yesterday. I didn't know when the last time Grunt or Snow went to the beach, so I was sure that they would appreciate the trip.

When everyone finally got to the beach I introduced everyone to each other, but that's when I found out that Tibby and Snow already knew each other. It was a little weird, but I guess I wanted them to be friends anyway, so it worked out pretty well.

We played in the water for a little bit, and I made sure to make the best pun that was said all day. I looked right at Snow and Tibby and said, "This water's pretty cold...I bet it must chill you right down to your bone." I did a dumb pun laugh, and Tibby and Snow splashed me. It was worth it.

Later, we had a sand castle building contest, Skeletons versus Zombies. I'm a little sad to say that Grunt and I lost that contest. We're not really artists or architects...so our castle just looked like a little hill. The girl's castle was actually really impressive, so they won, no questions asked. I bought them some ice cream as a prize.

Today was a really great day. I wish

that all days could be this good. At least
the weekend isn't over yet. I'm sure to do
something fun again tomorrow!

Day Twenty-Three: What Time is it? Bro Time.

Dear Diary,

I had a lot of fun at the beach the last couple of days, but now I think it's time for me to just chill for a little bit. After all, I do have to show up for my gym class tomorrow and I know that it's going to be a challenge day, so I might as well relax while I can. I can almost sense how tired my legs are going to be when I run the mile again tomorrow...I need to rest now in advance...and eat a lot of ice cream.

It's very important to my preparation process, probably.

Luckily, I knew someone who liked to chill more than anyone else I know-- Roarbert. I knocked on his bedroom door and waited for him to answer it. The moon had been up for hours, but it looked like he had just woken up. I never understood teenagers. How can they sleep until the middle of the night? It just doesn't make any sense.

Roarbert was a little mad that I woke up him, but he was too tired to kick my butt for it, so that was good. He said that we could hang out (after I asked him, Roarbert would never offer to hang out with me first) if I brought him some soda and snacks. I did what he asked, but only because I wanted soda and snacks too, not because he told me to.

I brought everything back to Roarbert's room and he threw on a movie. We didn't really talk much, but I didn't mind. It was just nice to relax and do nothing for once. I wish that I had time for more do-nothing days. One day, I hope that I can become rich so that I can pay other people to do stuff for me so that I never need to do anything again. I'll only do what I want to. That's how today worked until my mom made me take out the trash, but that wasn't too bad.

Anyway, I've got my gym class tomorrow, so I'm going to go to sleep now. I have a big day ahead of me, and I'm not really looking forward to it. I'll write more tomorrow.

Day Twenty-Four: The Beginning of Challenge Week

Dear Diary,

This gym class hasn't been nearly as bad as I thought it would be. They say that time flies when you're having fun, and I think the saying is true. It's the last week of gym class, and I didn't even realize it until today. I only noticed it because Mr. Inferno announced it to the whole class while he took attendance. He also announced one other thing. Today marked the start of challenge week, which isn't as bad as it sounds. We're going to play sports as challenges instead of doing push-ups, which isn't so bad.

Today was so bad, though. Today we had to run the mile again, but at least this would be the last time that I would have to do it. Once Mr. Inferno was done with his announcement everyone went outside and stood next to the starting line. He blew his whistle and everyone started to run.

I saw a few kids try to take the shortcut, but I knew better than to try to deal with that again. I kept to the trail and didn't cheat at all this time. It actually felt really good, I mean, until I had to jog uphill.

I knew that I was going to be graded on my time, but I hardly cared when I got to that hill. I could see the finish line at the top, but I didn't have the energy to run up it. By the looks of it, most of the other kids in my class didn't have the energy for it either. I knew that I couldn't give up, though. I walked up the hill. I was slow, but at least I was still moving.

Eventually, I got to the top of the hill and crossed the finish line. I didn't win the race or anything, but I wasn't last either, so I was pretty happy with myself. So, that makes one challenge day down and four to go. I think that I'm ready for it. I'll write all about the first real contest tomorrow.

Day Twenty-Five: Dodgeball Challenge

Dear Diary,

Today is the first real day of the challenge week. At least, it's the first real sport of the week. Of course, I wasn't happy to hear that the first real sport was my dreaded failure from the first week of class: dodgeball.

As soon as I heard about this I got really anxious. Bad memories about how I failed at this game last time made me worry that it was all just going to happen again. I just wanted to run home and get away from the game, but I knew that I needed to stay here if I was going to pass the fifth grade. Besides, Mr. Inferno already took attendance before he told us which game we were playing, so I know that he would notice if I took off before class ended. I had to stay here, even though I would have wanted to be literally anywhere else. I did hear that the Nether was nice around this time of year.

I knew I couldn't leave, so I had to force myself to stay. My friend Will was one of the team captains, so I asked him to pick me first for his team. Literally, almost everyone else in the class was better at this game than I was, but Will still picked me first, which made me feel really good about myself.

I was really nervous when the game actually started. I knew I was going to get out quickly, I just knew it. I was really surprised when I threw my first ball and it actually hit a kid. I was actually pretty stoked about it. I was so excited that I got distracted and some kid on the other team was able to throw a ball right at my gut. Man did that hurt.

Even with my loss, my team still won the game. It wasn't actually as bad as I thought it was going to be. At least I know that it only gets better from here on out. After all, dodgeball is my least favorite sport. Anything that we do tomorrow has to be better. Whatever we end up doing, I'll be sure to write all about it tomorrow.

Day Twenty-Six: Volleyball Challenge

Dear Diary,

I'm really beat today, so I don't think that I'm going to write very much today. Really, I'm just feeling pretty done. Done is probably the best way that I can describe how I'm feeling. It's like I just want to go to bed, but I'm not actually tired enough to sleep yet. I just want the day to be over. I guess since I'm feeling this way, I might as well write about why I'm feeling this way.

So, today was the second sports day

of challenge week. I thought that it couldn't really get any worse than dodgeball, but that's only because I forgot that I hated volleyball too. Well, I don't hate volleyball, but it's still not one of my better sports. I hope that eventually, we get around to the sports that I'm good at or else this challenge week isn't going to be fun at all.

I didn't get picked first for the team, or second, or third. I got picked fifth, and there were only seven kids on our team, so that about sums up how much people wanted to pick me, aka, they didn't really feel like picking me.

The game itself wasn't so good either. In the middle of a game, I ran to hit a ball, ended up bumping into someone, tripping, and then having the ball smack me in the face. It was a pretty rough moment, to say the least. Luckily, after that, I got to sit out because I was pretty sure that my nose was broken. I later found out that it wasn't, but it still hurt a lot.

Anyway, it should be clear to see that my day was pretty crummy, so I think I'm just going to sit around and watch TV for the rest of the day. I'll write more tomorrow if I even have the energy to do it.

Day Twenty-Seven: Baseball Challenge

Dear Diary,

I was actually happy to hear about today's challenge. We were going to be playing baseball today. I was pumped. Finally, I would get to play a sport that I was kind of good at. I mean, it wasn't fencing or anything, but it was still something that I liked.

I was on Will's team, which was pretty good. He's a pretty cool guy. He's okay at sports, which really helped our team's cause. I didn't get to be the pitcher today, but I did get to guard second base. I think it was a good base to guard. It was an important job, but not as important as guarding third base. I did a pretty good job at it too. I got Tibby out, which she didn't like too much, but my team liked it.

Guarding a base was okay, but I liked being up to bat even more. There was just something about a baseball coming straight at my face motivates me to hit it. I got a few strikes, but I did hit the ball more than I missed it...if that makes sense. I didn't get any home runs or anything, but I still did a good job.

If this match was going to get graded, I'm pretty sure that I'd get a B+ but I don't want to brag. I had to keep myself modest, that's just what super cool people like me do.

Anyway, I guess that tomorrow is Friday, which means it'll be the last day of challenge week and the last day of gym class...which means it'll be the last day of summer school! I hardly ever thought that day was going to come. I won't bother getting excited about it now. I will get excited when I write all about it tomorrow, though.

Day Twenty-Eight: Fencing Challenge

Dear Diary,

Challenge week couldn't have ended with a better sport. I love fencing. Even if I didn't learn anything else cool from this class I would still be happy because I got to learn all about fencing. Even after summer school is over I'm probably going to keep on fencing just for fun. Maybe I'll even start a fencing club of my own. Anyway, I really should focus on what actually happened today.

There were no teams today. It was

every mob for his/her/itself. If we were playing any other sport, I would have been super freaked out about being alone, but I was confident that I would be able to win.

The first round I had to face a kid named Goog. He wasn't very good at fighting, so I beat him right away. Goog had to sit out for the rest of the day, but I got to move onto the next level. There were going to be four levels in all. If I beat all of the levels then I would be the winner!

Next up was my friend Will. He was okay at the game, but I was always one step ahead of him. With a quick dash and a dodge, I was able to get out of his reach, but he wasn't as quick as me. I tapped him in the gut with my wooden sword. He was out. I won another round.

Next, up I had to find Cindy May. She was one of those girls who thought that she was super cool just because she had straight A's, even though she managed to flunk a gym class and land her way in summer school. She bragged about being really good at that stuff--it was annoying, but it was also true. I had a hard time keeping up with her, and there were a few narrow misses, but in the end, I was able to win!

It was finally time for the last round. I was up against Tibby. I knew she was good at sword fighting, but I didn't know that she was this good. As we were playing, her wooden sword hit me in one of my arms, so I had to pretend that it got cut off. I managed to hit her in the leg, though. She had to pretend it was cut off, so she was hopping all over the place. She swung and missed. I swung and hit. It was game over. I had won!

Well, I'm really tired from all of the fencing that I did today, so I'm just going to write more tomorrow. Even though I am tired, today was a really great last day of summer school.

Day Twenty-Nine: Party Time!

Dear Diary,

I got a letter from the school just this morning. Well, it wasn't from my elementary school. It was from the school that I would go to middle school at! That's right! I passed all of my summer school classes! Now I was going to go into middle school.

My parents were very proud of me for what my dad called, "getting my act together." They said that I could have as many friends as I wanted over, but I really only wanted to see Grunt and Snow. We had been so busy this last month that we hardly got to see each other. Besides, I just got done hanging out with all of my gym friends yesterday.

I really wanted to see my friends so that I could find out if they passed all of their classes. I was so nervous to find out that I almost didn't want to know. Luckily, my friends came to my house with some snacks and with their letters saying that they had passed their classes. I was so excited to hear the good news that I couldn't help to hug them until they needed to be let go for air. This was the best news I got all day! My friends and I were going to middle school together!

For our little party we watched some movies, ate all of the candy that we could without barfing, and we just talked about what we thought middle school was going to be like. Personally, I wasn't scared and neither was Snow. Grunt was a little nervous, but I knew that I would be there for him if he needed anything.

After the party, everyone went home and I had the place to myself. It was nice. I was home alone, me, Ugh the middle schooler. It feels nice to write. I'll write a little more tomorrow.

Day Thirty: Packing Up

Dear Diary,

This summer was kind of crazy. I would never have imagined that a summer filled only with school and a few weekends could be as crazy as this summer was. My friendship with Grunt had some ups and downs, and I made some great new friends like Snow, Tibby, and Will.

There's not much left for me to do this summer, other than to pack up my backpack for middle school. After all, I start sixth grade tomorrow. I'm not sure what it is going to be like, but I'm sure that I'll like it anyway. I know that with my friends by my side I can do anything that I put my mind to. Now I'll just have to remember not to skip class this year. Summer school was great and all, but I think that I'd rather hang out with my friends at the beach next summer.

I'm all ready for middle school now. I just hope that middle school is ready for me!

The Zombie Middle School Diary
Book 4: My Home Economics Teacher is a Pigman

Day One: The Last Day of Summer Vacation

Dear Diary,

My name is Ugh, and I've finally finished summer school. Of course, that just means that I need to start going to my normal school tomorrow. I'm a little nervous about it, but I'm mostly excited. I worked so hard to be able to get into middle school, and now I'm going to do my best in school this year so that I don't end up in summer school again.

When I was in fifth grade I was young and foolish. I skipped a lot of my classes to hang out with my pal Grunt, even though I could have just passed him notes during class...now that I think about it. Anyway, I'm not a slow learner or anything, but since I skipped so many classes I had to go to summer school for the WHOLE summer. Well, except for weekends, but it was still most of the summer.

I had a few crazy teachers while I was in summer school. I had this really cool history teacher. Her name was Ms. Skele and she was so old that she actually helped to make history. I had another teacher named Miss Enchantment. She was kind of strict, but I did learn a lot in her class. She was half-human and half-witch, which I didn't even know was possible. We learned how to make a mix of experiments and potions. It was actually really cool. My last teacher was a gym teacher. His name was Mr. Inferno. He was a Blaze, but he didn't have the temper of a Blaze. I wasn't very good in that class at first, but as time went on I got better. I actually made a couple friends in that class, too.

Speaking of my friends, they all passed summer school, too. That means that they'll be moving onto middle school with me! My best friend is Grunt. He's a zombie like me...and also a little bit of a slacker like me. I guess that's why we get along so well. My second best friend is Snow. We met in summer school. She's not a slow learner, either. She transferred schools in a weird part of the year, so she fell behind. She's actually pretty smart and cool for a girl Skeleton. Another girl Skeleton who I'm friends with is Tibby. I met her in my gym class. She's just as tough as any guy, but she still likes some girly stuff too. She's pretty cool. Lastly, I'm also friends with this guy named Will who I met in my gym class.

I can't wait to see all of my friends at school tomorrow. I hope it goes well. Whatever happens, I'll write all about it tomorrow!

Day Two: The First Day of Middle School

Dear Diary,

Today is the first day of middle school. I was so excited to go to school right away and put away my things in my locker. That's one cool new thing about middle school, having lockers. In elementary school, we had to keep all of our books in our desk. We sat in the same room all day with the same teacher. Now that we're in middle school we get to put all of our books in lockers, switch classrooms every once in a while and have a different teacher for every subject. It's a lot more complicated than elementary school, but I think it's going to be a lot more fun, too.

A lot of the kids were really tired today. I bet they weren't used to waking up as soon as the sun sets like I was. I was probably the most awake person around the place, and that's counting the teachers. Because of all of this, I didn't really get to talk to my friends much today. All they wanted to do was take naps, which was pretty lame.

I didn't even have to do much in class today, which was cool and boring at the same time. A lot of teachers handed out those syllabus things that Miss Enchantment gave me a couple months ago. We were just told what the rules were, what the homework was going to be like, and what would happen if we needed anything or if we broke the rules. The good news is that the teachers were so busy doing this that we didn't get any homework.

Today was kind of lame, but I'm sure that tomorrow will be cooler. When it is, I'll write all about it.

Day Three: Introducing...

Dear Diary,

I just realized today that I forgot to mention some important things in this diary, like who my teachers are and why I'm even writing this diary in the first place. I think I'm going to start with the latter.

So, in the summer my mom made me write in a diary as a bonus punishment for getting stuck in summer school. She didn't read it or anything, but she did make sure to check that I wrote something. Her eyesight is really bad, so whenever she did look at it, everything just looked really blurry to her. She's not making me write this diary, but I kind of liked writing in a diary in summer school, so I decided to keep it up, at least for a little bit. I don't know how long I'll be able to write in this thing before things get really busy at school, but I'm going to try to keep up on it for as long as I can.

Moving on to the other thing I wanted to write about, I have a lot of funky teachers this year. Miss Enchantment got a full-time job teaching here, so that's one familiar face, but none of my other summer school teachers are here. Most of the teachers were Skeletons or Zombies, so there's not really anything exciting to write about.

The teacher that really caught my attention was this pigman named Mr. Nocab who is teaching my home economics class. He's probably the fattest pigman that I've ever seen. I don't know why the principal put him in charge of food. I mean, he'll probably just end up eating it all. He just looks like the sort of guy who could get in some sort of silly problems, like a cartoon character that keeps bumping into stuff and who does everything wrong. I think I'll actually write about how that class goes tomorrow. I bet it'll be hilarious.

Day Four: Home Ec? More Like Hilarious Ec.

Dear Diary,

The first few days of my home ec class were mostly just safety tips like, don't cut yourself when you're cutting food, don't do this, don't do that, blah, blah, blah. It was all pretty boring. Nothing funny happened at all. Today was the first day that the class actually did anything, so I was just waiting for something silly to happen. Let's just say that I did not leave the room feeling disappointed.

Today we went out into the school's garden to learn how to know when the plants were ready to pick. Luckily, the school's garden was pretty big so everyone got to pick some stuff. It was actually kind of fun to get my hands dirty to pick stuff, but that wasn't the funny part about all of this.

The funny part of the class happened when I caught Mr. Nocab munching on some of the carrots that he had just pulled out of the ground. I go to school at night, but since I'm a zombie I can still see pretty well in the dark. I was able to see that Mr. Nocab took the carrot out of the dirt and then just ate it! He didn't even try to wipe off the dirt or anything! It was gross.

The grossest part of all of this was that he didn't even do it just once. Whenever he thought that someone wasn't looking he would pick up another carrot and just eat it right there. With every bite, he took I could hear him chomping down on the crunchy carrot. I'm sure that everyone else could hear it, too.

When it was time to eat after class almost all of the kids were doing something to make fun of what Mr. Nocab had done. Some kids were chomping on carrots extra hard, and I even saw one kid dip his carrots into chocolate pudding to pretend it was dirt. It was gross but really funny. I knew this class would be great for some laughs.

I'll make sure to write some more super funny stuff tomorrow.

Day Five: Snow and Tibby's Adventures

Dear Diary,

I don't know if I ever mentioned it before, but Skeletons don't really need to eat unless they want to, and a big part of home ec is learning how to cook different things. Because of all of these things, Tibby and Snow aren't in my home ec class. We have some other classes together, but we can pretty much only hang out when it's time to eat. Man...do I miss recess right about now.

Anyway, Snow and Tibby wanted to tell us about the class that they were in since they didn't have to suffer through home ec with Mr. Nocab like Will, Grunt, and I had to. They had to take a class that was made just for Skeletons. It kind of sounded like they were doing arts and crafts, but they weren't doing any baby stuff like finger painting (bone painting?) or anything like that.

From how they explained it, they were making art like how Skeletons used to make art before they merged in with monster society. It was all very...cultural. It was actually kind of neat. Tibby said that they would eventually learn how to make their own bows and arrows. I was pretty jealous of their class. It sounded like it was going to be a lot more fun than this home ec class that I was stuck in. I wonder if I could disguise myself as a Skeleton...I probably couldn't. I don't have much meat on me, but I have way too much to look like a Skeleton.

Anyway, I promised to write about something funny, but nothing super funny happened today. I found a joke in a book I was reading today, so I'll just write that instead: What did the human say to the angry Creeper? "Looks like you've got an explosive temper!"

I'm sure something funnier will happen tomorrow so I don't need to make up my own jokes. I'll write more then.

Day Six: The Assembly

Dear Diary,

  While I was sitting in my homeroom classroom today there was an announcement that went out on the speakers in every room. "The club assembly will begin in five minutes. Anyone who is interested in joining a club or team may leave their homeroom at this time." Was I super interested in joining a club right now? Nah. Was I super interested in ditching homeroom? Yeah. Maybe my class skipping ways coming back to haunt me? I hope not. Besides, this time, I have a real excuse. I just need to make sure not to make a bad habit of it.

It seemed like all of my friends were interested in checking out the clubs too, so we all left the room together and made our way down to the gym where the clubs were going to be setting up their stuff. When I got there I just saw tables and tables full of flyers and free pens. I hadn't thought about joining a club up until now, but seeing how many clubs my school had made me kind of want to join a club.

Eventually, my friends caught up to me and we looked around at the tables together to see if there was anything we would want to join. Within minutes the girls broke off from the group to look into some Skeleton-only clubs, so I was left with just Grunt and Will to hang out with.

My guy friends can be a bit mean sometimes, I'm not going to lie. All of the mocking started when we passed the cooking club table. Who was sitting in the chair behind the table? None other than

Mr. Nocab himself. "I dare you to sign up for the cooking class," Grunt said.

"How is there even going to be a cooking class with Mr. Nocab running it? He'll just eat everything before it gets cooked," Will said.

"You mean like those carrots he was chomping on the other day?" I added in. We had a good laugh.

I didn't really see any clubs I was super into, but I think I'll probably sign up for something anyway just to get involved with something. I guess there was a pretty cool Zombies-only club that sounded a lot like the cool art class Snow and Tibby were taking. I think I might sign up for that later. I'll do my best to remember, but right now I've got to go back to class. I'll write more tomorrow.

Day Seven: Talking with Roarbert

Dear Diary,

My big brother Roarbert doesn't know a lot about anything other than video games and pizza, so I don't really ask for his advice on a lot of things. Of course, I do ask him what to do when I really need his help, like when Grunt and I used to argue a lot during summer school, but since then I haven't really needed to talk to him about much. Granted, summer school did end about a week ago, so I guess I might actually ask for his advice more than I would like to think I do.

Today I wanted to ask him about something that he had a few years of experience on, and that I didn't. Roarbert is a few years older than me, so he just finished middle school last year. I knew that this meant he was busy dealing with the complicated problems of high school, but I figured that he could at least give me some advice on how to act during my three years in middle school.

I knocked on Roarbert's door and asked if I could ask him something. To this, he only replied, "You just did ask me something," and slammed the door. Man, teenagers sure can be annoying sometimes. I knocked on his door again and told him that it was important, and he finally let me in.

"What's up little bro?" He asked him. I didn't like it when he called me little bro. It made me feel like I was a baby or something.

"I was wondering if you could give me some advice on middle school," I felt dumb saying it out loud, but if anyone could help me with this I knew it would be Roarbert.

"I've actually been waiting for you to ask me this," Roarbert said. This surprised me, mostly because I didn't know that Roarbert knew how to wait for anything. Then again, he's surprised me before. "I can see that you're gonna set yourself up for failure."

"Geez, thanks," I told him. He really wasn't helping.

"I didn't mean it like that. I mean it like...how do I put it? You were kind of a slacker in elementary school, and I know that you're not going to do that again. You just try to act cool and tough, and that's not going to get you anywhere in middle school."

"It's not?" I asked. I guess I did kind of have a tough guy routine in elementary school.

"It's not. You need to be yourself. I know that it sounds like something that Mom would say, but it's true. You'll make way more friends that way and get into less trouble. If you just do that, then you'll be fine."

"What if I'm actually a tough guy, though?" I asked him.

Roarbert punched me in the arm and I yelled something that I don't want to write in here. "You're not a tough guy," he said. I guess he proved me wrong.

At least I got what I wanted out of him. I guess that Roarbert's good for something, even if his words of advice come with a bruise every once in a while.

Day Eight: Zombie Meets Overworld

Dear Diary,

I know that I asked Roarbert for advice, but he only gave me one thing of it. I didn't even know if it was good advice. I did know of one great source for advice about middle school: Zombie Meets Overworld.

One of my favorite shows is called Zombie Meets Overworld. It's about this great Zombie who gets into all kind of mischief with his friends at school. At the end of every episode, there's always some sort of lesson that the characters are supposed to learn. I figured that I could watch a few episodes of it today to figure out if Roarbert's advice is real or not. I'll write more after I watch some of this show.

***

After watching the first full season, I feel like my eyes are going to fall out. However, I also feel like I learned 23 new lessons. A lot of the lessons actually seem to match up with what Roarbert said the other day. I think that I'll take his advice and try to be less of a tough guy during middle school. Besides, if I don't act like such a slacker, I might make some new friends or something. I don't really know what will happen, but I'm willing to give it a try.

Anyway, I'm pretty tired from watching TV all day, so I'm going to bed now. Since I have school tomorrow, I'm sure that I'll have something more exciting to write about than just watching TV all day.

Day Nine: Sewing

Dear Diary,

My home ec class was so dumb today. I had to sit there, just sewing all day. I mean, when am I ever going to need to learn how to sew. Only girls do that sort of thing. I mean, I've never seen my dad or Roarbert sew. My mom is in charge of all of that stuff. I'll probably never have to sew again in my life. Boys shouldn't need to learn how to do it.

One thing I did learn today is that girls really hate it when a boy says that something is only for girls. I mean, I thought girls wanted more stuff to themselves. I mean, boys get sports and manly stuff life that, shouldn't girls be happy that they get sewing and whatever other lame stuff they like? Of course, saying pretty much what I just wrote down in my diary during my home ec class taught me that girls don't like that.

Saying that something is only for girls or only for boys gets girls really mad. I mean, I mentioned this to a girl...and it didn't go well. I mean, there was even a hard punch in the mix. I didn't hit her or anything, but she socked me right in the gut. I didn't know what "you hit like a girl" meant until today, but I'm not sure why anyone uses it as an insult. It hurt! Luckily, the girl who punched me got kicked out of class, but so did I.

I still don't understand why that girl got so mad. I think I'm going to talk to Snow and Tibby about it tomorrow. At least they're two girls who like me. Now I

just have to hope that they aren't as prone
to hitting as Miss Punchy McPunch-fist
was in my class today. I'll write about what
I discover tomorrow. I'm sure it'll help
confused boys everywhere. At least, it'll
help them from getting punched...

Day Ten: A Meal with the Girls

Dear Diary,

I wanted to find out what made a girl tick, or I guess, what I said to make a girl so ticked off at me. Luckily, I had two great friends who also happened to be girls. I figured if anyone could tell me what was wrong, without totally hating me after telling me what was wrong, it would be Tibby and Snow.

I sat with the girls when it was time to eat. Grunt and Will were off doing something else, so I had Tibby and Snow all to myself. I didn't really know how to bring up my questions to them. In the end, I just ended up telling them what happened yesterday. When I was done telling them what happened yesterday, I asked them, "So what about what I said do you think made that girl so mad?"

At the same time, Tibby and Snow said, "Everything." This answer didn't really bring me any closer to understanding what exactly I did wrong.

Luckily, Snow explained what 'everything' meant. "Girls have had to deal with that sort of garbage language since forever. It's really annoying. I mean, it's pretty much the future now. There aren't really boy or girl things anymore. Girls can like sports and video games. Boys can like cooking and they need to learn how to sew, even if you don't think that it's super important."

I think I got what Snow was saying, but I was still confused on one thing. "If girls don't like it when people talk like I did, then how come a bunch of people talk like I did all of the time?"

It was Tibby who answered this time. "Well, girls used to only do some things, but it was mostly because boys made them. Since it kept happening, boys thought that girls liked that sort of thing, and girls thought it was their job to like stuff like playing with dolls and cleaning up. Things are changing now. Boys are allowed to like things that only girls supposed to like and vice versa."

"When a boy says that something is only for girls or that he shouldn't have to do it because he's a boy, it makes it sound like boys are better than girls, which isn't true. Everyone should be treated equally, whether they're a girl or boy. Everyone should learn how to cook because everyone needs to eat, and stuff like that. It's just common sense." Once Snow said this, I realized that it was common sense.

I'm going to learn to treat girls and boys the same way. It might take a little while to get used to it, but I'm going to do my best. I'm glad that I have Tibby and Snow to talk to about this sort of stuff. I wouldn't trade them for the coolest dudes in all of Overworld.

Day Eleven: Signing Up

Dear Diary,

I totally forgot about the club thing. I wanted to join a club, but I forgot to look into them more after the assembly thing. I couldn't even remember what all of the clubs were, but it was the last day to sign up for one, so I had to pick one soon. It was now or never.

The only club that I could actually remember talking about was the cooking club. I mean, I know that Grunt, Will, and I only talked about it because they wanted to dare me to join it, but it doesn't actually seem like that bad of a club. I mean, sure, Mr. Nocab was teaching the club, but he wasn't really a bad guy either. He was just kind of silly in class sometimes.

After the talk that the girls and I had yesterday, I don't think that joining a cooking club would be such a bad thing. After all, Snow did mention that everyone needed to learn how to cook, whether they were a boy or girl didn't really matter.

Luckily, there was still a lot of room on the sign-up sheet when I got to it. I signed my name up for the cooking class. I think it'll actually be pretty cool, but if Grunt or Will asks, I'm going to say that I just did it because of the dare. Even though I know that guys can like cooking, I'm not sure that they know. I don't want to get made fun of. I just want to make a cake.

Anyway, I'm super busy today, so I'll just write some more tomorrow.

Day Twelve: A Sewing Situation

Dear Diary,

Nothing exciting happened at school today, but I know that something cool will happen in a couple days. This weekend I'm going to have my twelfth birthday! I've been so busy with school that I didn't even have time to snoop around the house to look for my birthday present from my parents. Luckily, today I didn't have any homework and my parents were going out. It was my chance to strike!

My parents had a few hiding places

for presents, but I knew where all of them were. Luckily, my parents didn't know that I knew where they were, so I never had to look very hard to find my presents. Sure, it took away some of the surprise value, but finding it on my own is way more fun than being surprised anyway.

It didn't take me too long to find a party bag with my name on it. I looked inside of the bag and saw a cool leather jacket. I have wanted one of these for a while now, and I'm actually a little impressed that my parents remembered that I wanted one. I took it out of the bag and tried it on. I looked pretty good in it if I have to say so myself.

There was I flexing my huge muscles when it happened. The jacket ripped. I mean, it was a really obvious rip. I knew that I would be in deep trouble if my parents found out. At first, I was panicking pretty hard. I mean, I had no idea what to do. Then I remembered what I learned in class.

I ran into my parent's room and pulled out my mom's sewing kit. I tried my best to remember what I learned in class and stitched up the jacket the best I could. It didn't look like new when I was done, but it looked good enough. When I was done fixing the jacket I put it back in the party bag and then back in its hiding spot.

I'm safe...for now. I'll write more tomorrow if my mom doesn't find out about my sneaking around. If that happens...then I'll be grounded until my next birthday!

Day Thirteen: Behaving Better

Dear Diary,

I have definitely learned my lesson. Everyone should learn how to sew. At least, everyone should know how to not snoop around for their birthday presents. However, I think I'm too stuck in the habit of snooping to get over it. At least I know how to fix what I ruin. I'm just glad that I didn't break something electrical. I would have no idea how to fix something like that.

Since I have proof that sewing is an

important skill, I tried to do my best in home ec today. I mean, I even paid attention, participated, and everything like that. I was a perfect student. Well, I guess I was an average student, but that's still better than how I usually act. I didn't get into any fights or anything.

Anyway, today wasn't super exciting, so that's about all I have to write about today. Tomorrow will be more fun to write about because I'm going to have a birthday party. It's going to be sweet. I'll write all about it tomorrow.

Day Fourteen: Happy Birthday to Me!

Dear Diary,

My birthday party was just as cool as I thought it would be! I invited Snow, Tibby, Grunt, and Will to my party. No one was busy, so they were all able to make it. I was a little worried that someone might be busy, but I was glad to know that everyone could make it. Even Roarbert came out of his room to help me celebrate, or maybe he just came out of his room because he could smell the pizza, either way, he was there too.

I've never turned twelve before, so I wasn't really sure what people are supposed to do at twelve-year-old birthday parties. I mean, I'm the oldest out of all of my friends, and Roarbert didn't invite me to his party, so I didn't really know what to do.

I opened my presents first. I got a lot of really cool stuff for my gifts. I made to sure act super surprised when I got the jacket from my parents. I was even more surprised to see that Roarbert got me a present. He got me my very own fencing sword! It was just made out of wood, but it was good enough for me. I guess that Will was in on this too because he got me a sword too. Now I could fight with my friends...but in a good way! Grunt got me some trading cards for a game we like to play. Snow baked me the best brownies that I've ever had, and Tibby got me a cool baseball cap with our school's logo on it.

Luckily, one of my birthday presents (from my grandparents, who sent it through the mail because they couldn't make it to my party) was two extra controllers for my video game system. Now I had enough for everyone to play video games at the same time. I actually had a great game that everyone could play together called Super Monster Party. I guess, in a way, my birthday party was a super monster party.

I wish that I could relive this day over and over, that's how great it was. I know that I can't do that. Besides, writing about this every day would get pretty boring. I'll write some more tomorrow, though, about whatever it is that I get up to.

Day Fifteen: Time to Chill

Dear Diary,

The party yesterday sure did take a lot out of me. I kind of just wanted to chill out today. Usually, I would invite my friends over on a weekend, but I saw so much of them yesterday that I just wanted to hang out at home alone. Sometimes a guy just needs some alone time.

I decided to look over the presents I got yesterday. I even wore my new jacket all day, and it wasn't even that cold outside. I looked pretty cool in this jacket, though.

If I was a little older, I'm sure that all of the ladies in Overworld would think I'm the coolest guy around.

Eventually, I got bored of imagining my future modeling career, so I decided to see if Roarbert wanted to hang out. Sure, a guy needs a little alone time every now and again, but a lot of alone time can get pretty boring. I knocked on his door and asked him if he wanted to play some video games. He agreed to play with me, but probably only because he's not that too good looking to even pretend that he has a future as a male model.

My day was pretty tame today. I played some video games and ate a lot of left-over pizza and cake. It was pretty good. I have to go back to school tomorrow, which I'm not really looking forward to. It's too bad that school can't just be like a big party, then I'd want to go every day. I guess I'll just write about the lack of a party at school tomorrow.

Day Sixteen: The Cooking Club

Dear Diary,

Today was the first day of the cooking club. I'm not really even sure why I showed up to the club. I mean, I only signed up for it on a dare and because all of the other clubs were full. I could have skipped the meeting and no one would have even noticed.

I showed up anyway, and now I'm kind of glad that I did. I sat down in the kitchen and waited for Mr. Nocab to show up. There were a few other kids in the class already. Most of the people in the club were girls, but there were two other boys in the club, too.

Today Mr. Nocab was going to teach us how to bake muffins. The whole thing seemed a lot like our home ec class, except it was a lot more relaxed. Mr. Nocab was throwing around jokes left and right. It was actually pretty fun. We got to make whatever kind of muffins that we wanted. A lot of kids stuck to blueberries and chocolate chips, but I decided to throw in a bag of chocolate candies and marshmallows into my muffins. When they were done they tasted a lot more like cake than muffins, but they were still good.

I'm actually pretty glad that I showed up to this club. It was a lot more fun than I thought it would be. I guess the joke is really on Will and Grunt for not signing up for this club. I'm sure that I'll show up for the next meeting, whether I really need to or not.

Day Seventeen: Other Clubs

Dear Diary,

Since my club meeting went so well yesterday, I wanted to hear all about how well my friend's meetings went. We had all pretty much signed up for different things, except for Snow and Tibby, who had both signed up for the archery club. I guess that's just the sort of thing that cool skeletons gals are into nowadays.

Grunt and Will didn't join the same team. They actually didn't hang out all that often. I mean, they were both friends with me, so they hung out together when I was around, but they didn't really hang out alone together. Anyway, they were pretty different people. Grunt ended up signing up for the bowling club, which I think he just did as an excuse to go to the bowling alley once a week. Will signed up for an art class. Until today I didn't even know that he was into art. I guess I learn something new about my friends every day.

I also made sure to tell my friends all about the cooking club meeting. They actually seemed a little impressed. At first, they thought it was funny that I actually showed up for the meeting, but by the time that I was done telling them all about the meeting they wished that they had joined the club instead of making jokes about it.

Anyway, that's about all that I've got to write about today. I bet that I'll have something cool to write about tomorrow, though, so I'll make sure to write more then.

Day Eighteen: Club Meets Classroom

Dear Diary,

Today my home ec club was moving onto something that I already had a little bit of experience with cooking. I was glad that I joined the cooking class now. I had a little advantage over the other kids in the class. We weren't baking muffins like I did in my class, but we were making homemade bread, which was basically the same thing. I was all out of candy to throw into the bread, though, so I just had to go by the recipe that Mr.

Nocab had written on the board for everyone to use.

Some of the other kids in the class kept getting some stuff mixed up in the recipe. I mean, some kid put in a whole cup of salt in their mixing bowl instead of a cup of flour. If I hadn't had helped out that kid then his bread would have tasted really gross.

A lot of the kids in class were actually impressed with how well I did when I was done with my bread. It was probably the fluffiest bread that was made in the whole class. Even Mr. Nocab liked my bread. He asked if I could share it with the whole class, and I agreed. It felt really good to have everyone enjoy something that I made all by myself.

I think I'm really starting to like my home ec class. I wonder what I'll get up to tomorrow. No matter what I do, I'll be sure to write all about it tomorrow!

Day Nineteen: Kitchen Tutor

Dear Diary,

Yesterday I did super well in my home ec class. I must have looked like a professional chef or like one of those people who were probably chefs once but now they're too old to work in a real kitchen so they just have a cooking show on public cable channels. Either way, I was way better cook than a lot of the kids in my class, and I was WAY better at cooking than Grunt and Will.

To tell the truth...Grunt and Will

aren't good at cooking, like at all. Before this class, the most complicated thing that Will had ever made was a grilled cheese, and I'm not even sure that Grunt knows how to make his own toast. Anyway, at the end of the week, our home ec class is going to have a cooking test, like a bake-off or something, and Grunt and Will asked me if I could tutor them so they would pass the test. I agreed to help out of the goodness of my heart, and also for the free snacks that they were paying me with.

I decided to help my friends make some brownies, partially because they were made pretty much like cake, but mostly I helped them make brownies because I really wanted to eat some brownies. I dug around my kitchen and found a recipe that my grandma had given my mom. It was the best brownie recipe I knew of. If they were going to make anything good, then this would be it.

We made the recipe together. I had to stop Grunt from throwing in the whole egg into the bowl instead of cracking it first, and Will almost forgot to add the chocolate to the brownies, which is kind of the most important part of brownies.

By the time the brownies were done, they smelled just like how my grandma made them. They didn't taste as good as my grandma made them, but it's impossible to make anything as good as my grandma made them. I would say that we did a pretty good job.

I'll write more tomorrow if I don't get sick from eating all of these brownies today.

Day Twenty: The Bake Sale Bake Off

Dear Diary,

Today was the day of the cooking test. Every student in the home ec class could make whatever they wanted. Everyone who made something that wasn't totally disgusting would get an A, but whoever sold the most of whatever they made would get a special prize. I was ready to win that prize. I didn't know what it was, but I knew that I wanted it.

I decided to make a batch of chocolate chip cookies. A person could never go wrong when it came to these cookies. They were super easy to make, and they always sold the fastest at bake sales. I was sure to win. My grandma didn't have a recipe for this but my mom did, so I decided to take it to school today to make my masterpiece.

I went to my cooking station in the home ec room and made the cookie dough, cut most of it into cookie shapes, and put it in the oven. Of course, I kept some of the cookie dough to eat raw while the rest of it was cooking. I know I'm not supposed to eat cookie dough, but it's just so good. I can't help myself.

When my cookies were done I put them on a plate and put them on the bake sale table. Once all of the other kid's stuff was out the sale started. I had competition, though. Someone else had made chocolate chip cookies. I pushed my plate to the front of the table to try to sell them faster. Luckily, my plan worked.

My cookies sold faster than

anything else. I won the secret prize super faster, which meant that my reward was huge! It turned out that my reward was getting one free snack from everyone's desserts. I got twelve different treats! Today was probably the best day of my life. Of course, I shared my snacks with my friends, but I kept the best snacks for myself.

There's no way tomorrow is going to be better than today, but I'll write about it anyway.

Day Twenty-One: Boys Only!

Dear Diary,

It's finally Saturday! It's the best day of the week, as far as I'm concerned. On Friday there's still school, on Sunday I need to get ready for school, but on Saturday all I need to do is relax and PARTY!

I invited over Grunt and Will to have a sleepover with me today. Middle school is a lot busier than I thought it would be. My friends and I don't have as much time as we used to for hanging out

333

as we did in elementary school. Today was going to be a boy's only day.

Roarbert was at a sleepover with his friends, so my friends and I had the whole place to ourselves, well, not counting my parents. I didn't know what to do with my friends. We just decided to do everything that we could think of. We played video games, played board games, and even baked stuff together. This cooking club and home ec class is really making me appreciate the finer arts of making and eating snacks. My mom took a lot of pictures of me cooking. She thought it was cute. I thought it was embarrassing.

Anyway, I had a great time with my friends. I'm going to hang out with Snow and Tibby tomorrow since I didn't hang out with either of them today. I'm sure it'll be pretty cool, and I'll make sure that I write all about it.

Day Twenty-Two: A Day Out with the Girls

Dear Diary,

Since I hung out with my bros yesterday, I figured that today would be a great time to hang out with my girl friends. It's very important that I keep that space between the word 'girl' and 'friends'. I only like Snow and Tibby as friends. I only like all girls as friends right now. I mean, I'm twelve. I don't need to start thinking about getting a girlfriend until I'm at least thirteen. Having girls who are my friends is cool, though.

I let the girls pick what we should do today. When Tibby said, "We should go to the mall," I was a little grossed out. Every boy knows that it means when a girl wants to go to a mall. It means that the boy will go in, and then never come out because he'll die of boredom while the girl shops. Of course, I did tell the girls they could pick, so I agreed to go with them.

Snow's mom drove us to the mall in the next village over. "This mall is way cooler than the one that we have in our village," Snow said. "It's way bigger. There're way more stores to shop at." I tried my very best not to complain. I thought about the ten gold blocks in my inventory. I hoped it would be enough to buy something.

The mall was a lot bigger than I thought it would be. It was also really clean, which is kind of weird for monster buildings. I mean, there was spider webs all over the place, but I guess that's just what a mall is asking for when they hire giant spiders for janitors. As I looked around the store, I noticed just how many stores there were, and how not all of them were clothes stores. The place wasn't actually as bad as I thought it was going to be.

The girls did want to do some shopping for clothes, but while they did that they made sure to point out a video game store me to look in so I didn't get bored. That store was actually really cool. A lot of the video games were old and used, but that also meant that they were pretty cheap. I was able to get a game that came out two years ago for only three gold blocks! When the game was new it would have been close to ten gold blocks!

I met up with the girls later and we went to a toy shop. I bought some mini blocks to play with. I can build a replica of my house when I get home if I want to. After that, the girls showed me the arcade. That was the best part of the whole mall. I have to admit that I used up the rest of the money here. Luckily, Snow's mom had given us money for dinner, so I didn't go hungry.

We got some burritos from the food court and waited outside for Snow's mom to pick us up. I had a really good time. I'm starting to think that I'll ask the girls to go to the mall with me more often, as soon as I get my allowance. Today was a really good day. I'll make sure to write more tomorrow.

Day Twenty-Three: The Cooking Club, Again

Dear Diary,

Today is Monday, which sadly meant that I needed to go to school today, but it also meant that I was able to go to the cooking club meeting. I know that I signed up for this club on a dare, but I'm actually really glad that I signed up for it. I mean, Mr. Nocab is a lot cooler during the club than during class. We also got to make a lot cooler stuff. Today we were learning how to make ice cream!

Mr. Nocab made everyone group up. I partnered up with a pigman named Tyler. He was pretty cool. All of the kids were handed two bags. We had a little bag for ice cream and a bigger bag for ice. I had to mix milk, sugar, and a tiny bit of salt into a bag. Then I was allowed to choose a flavor. A lot of kids picked vanilla, but I thought that was lame. I put in chocolate syrup and chocolate chips into my bag.

Once everything was in the bag, Tyler and I put both of our bags into the ice bag. We had to also add salt to the ice, which I guess made it even colder. I was wondering why we needed to have partners as I rolled the ice cream bag inside of the ice bag, but it didn't take me long to figure it out as I tried to make the ice cream. The ice bag got super cold. I gave it to Tyler to use, and we kept switching when we got too cold.

By the end of class, everyone was eating ice cream out of their bags. Mine didn't work as well as the vanilla kids, but it was worth it for every chocolatey bite. I'm going to finish eating this ice cream and then clean up. I'll make sure to write more tomorrow and maybe even make some more ice cream at home.

Day Twenty-Four: Grunt's Grunts

Dear Diary,

Something weird was up today, and I don't even know what it is. It's about Grunt, not me. I'm fine. It's just that every once in a while, Grunt gets really upset about something. He bottles up his feelings and then he takes it out on other people later. Grunt and I almost stopped being friends during the summer school program because he got jealous that I was doing better than him in class. I mean, I'm doing better than him in class right now, but I don't think he's mad at me for that. He hasn't said anything about it, anyway.

I could tell that something was up with Grunt, but Grunt didn't seem to want to tell me what was up with him. I even made sure to ask him directly, "Are you feeling okay?" instead of trying to be sneaky and figure out what was wrong. Grunt said that he was fine, but I don't think that he's telling the truth.

I'm going to wait for Grunt to tell me what is wrong on his own. It's rude to try to force someone to tell you what's wrong, and it only makes friendships more complicated. I know that Grunt will tell me what is wrong once he's ready to. I guess that I'll just have to wait until he feels ready to tell me what is wrong. I hope that Grunt knows that he can tell me whatever he needs to. That's just what best friends are for.

I'll write more tomorrow if Grunt tells me anything. Until he does, the best I can do is be patient with him.

Day Twenty-Five: Roarbert's Brotherly Advice

Dear Diary,

Grunt still hasn't said anything about what's bothering him, but he was definitely still acting like there was something wrong. I still haven't talked to him about whatever it is that's bothering him because I don't really know how to talk to him about his troubles. It's never gone super well when I've tried to talk to Grunt when something is going on with him. He's not exactly the best listener, especially when he gets his mind stuck on something. He's the most stubborn friend that I have, that's for sure.

I didn't really know how to talk to Grunt, but I did know how to talk to Roarbert. He was always around to give me advice when I needed it, and he was really good at giving me advice about Grunt, which was probably because half the time I needed advice it was so that I could learn how to talk to Grunt better. I wonder if Grunt ever asks for advice about how to talk to me.

I went into Roarbert's room and told him all about what was going on with Grunt. I asked him what he should do about the whole thing. He didn't have much to say, but what he said was important. "It actually seems like you're handling this really well. I think you should just keep doing what you're doing." Roarbert paused for a minute before finishing his thought. "You know, you've gotten a lot more mature since you started middle school. Pretty soon you won't even need my advice."

I left Roarbert's room after talking to him. It felt pretty good to get some props from my big brother. I think that Roarbert and I are getting to be better friends every day. Maybe I really am growing up and getting more mature.

Day Twenty-Six: Finally Talking

Dear Diary,

I knew that I should be patient, but being patient is really hard sometimes. I was so curious about whatever was bugging Grunt. I might have also been a little worried that he was mad at me for something. I couldn't really think of anything that I could have done to make him mad at me, but with a guy like Grunt, I can never be sure that I didn't do something. I was actually just about to straight up ask Grunt what was wrong when he walked up to me and shyly said,

"Can I talk to you about something?" Grunt had never been shy about anything since I met him. I knew that this was important. Grunt was finally about to open up to me.

We walked away from everyone else at school so we could be alone. Once Grunt knew that there was no one else around he said, "I'm really stressed out about something, and I need to talk to someone about it. Is it okay if I tell you?"

I felt touched that Grunt would come to me first. "Yeah, you can always tell me anything, you know that."

Grunt continued. "It's just this whole middle school thing. There's so much more work than in elementary school. I'm having a really hard time keeping up and my grades are getting really low. I'm just worried that if I don't get my grades back up I'll have to go to summer school again."

I understood what Grunt was

talking about. Even if my grades were not dropping, I still knew that middle school was a lot harder than elementary school. "I get it, man, school is getting pretty hard. Is there anything I can do to help?" I wanted to help Grunt, really, but I didn't know how I could help him.

"I know I need some help, but I don't really know what could help. I'm just too stressed out to think of any ideas. Do you...do you think that you could think of some way to help me out?" Grunt sounded really nervous when he asked me this.

"Yeah, I'll try to think of something and get back to you tomorrow, okay?" I pretended to know what I was doing. I hope that Grunt couldn't tell that I was just as clueless as he was.

"Thanks, bro," he said as he left.

It meant a lot to me that Grunt could talk to me about his troubles, but now I'm a little nervous. I don't really know how to help him out with his troubles. I'll try to sleep on it. I'll write about whatever I figure out tomorrow...if I can even figure out something.

Day Twenty-Seven: Summer Memories and Autumn Ideas

Dear Diary,

I don't know if other people get this, but sometimes when I'm trying to sleep I start thinking about stuff that I usually wouldn't think of, like really good food that I had years ago or about that time I fell off a slide and scraped my knee when I was in third grade. Last night I thought of something that could actually help Grunt out, though!

I was thinking about that time I

messed up in my chemistry class during summer school. I don't know why I was thinking about this, I just was. Anyway, when I messed up Miss Enchantment made me go to tutoring. I didn't really like it at first, but it really helped my grades and my stress. I think that the same thing can help Grunt.

I told Grunt about this when I got to school today. He didn't seem thrilled at the idea of signing up for tutoring, but he didn't fight me on it, either. He knew that he needed this, even if he didn't actually want to do it. I came with him to sign up for tutoring in general since Grunt needed help in most subjects. I even signed up for tutoring in math, partially to be nice and partially because that was my worst class.

Grunt was really glad that I had this idea, and he was even happier that I joined tutoring with him. I really think that I'm doing a good job at this whole middle school thing. I'll write some more about it tomorrow.

Day Twenty-Eight: Fencing

Dear Diary,

Signing up for tutoring was pretty stressful for Grunt, and it was even a little stressful for me. I didn't want to think about school today, and I don't think Grunt wanted to think about it, either. We needed to blow off some steam, and I knew the perfect way to do that.

In my last month of summer school, I had to take a gym class. I thought it was going to be really lame, but I actually had a lot of fun. I found out that I was really bad at some sports. I'm probably the worst playing volleyball. I also found some sports that I liked, my favorite being fencing, which is pretty much a fancy way to say sword fighting.

I had gotten some wooden swords for my birthday, so I offered to fight Grunt in my backyard with him. It was going to be for fun, obviously. We were trying to blow off some steam, not beat up each other.

We were sword fighting for a really long time, actually. I was trying to train Grunt how to be better at it with some of the stuff that I had learned in my gym class. By the time that we were done play-fighting Grunt had gotten a lot better. He wasn't better than me, but I did let him win a match to make him feel better.

Today was a pretty good day, and I'm not just saying that because I hustled Grunt and got him to buy me pizza after I beat him at fencing. The weekend isn't over yet, though! I'll make sure to write some more tomorrow.

Day Twenty-Nine: PARTY!

Dear Diary,

The first month of middle school is over! It seems like it lasted forever. I need something to celebrate...I needed to party, which is exactly what I did today! I invited all of my friends to meet me at the park: Snow, Will, Grunt, and Tibby all showed up. Tibby even brought an extra friend to join us. I think his name is Cranium. I didn't really talk to him much, but he seemed like a cool guy. I think there's something weird going on between Tibby and Cranium. That's not important right now, though.

What is important? The party! Like any cool middle school kid party, our party mostly consisted of the six of us standing around in the circle, talking about what shows we liked on TV, and eating more junk food than we probably should have. It was a pretty tame party, but I also can't really think of a better way to end the first month of middle school.

There's a teacher in-service tomorrow, so I don't have to go to school, which will give me some extra time to write. I'm not sure what to write about. I'm running out of paper in this diary, so I'll probably have to start a new one for next month. Of course, I'll make sure to put one last cool entry in this one, but I'll do that tomorrow. Right now, I've got a party to get back to.

Day Thirty: What Next?

Dear Diary,

There's only really one thing that's going through my mind right now, and that question is, what's going to happen next? I mean, I know that I survived my first month of middle school, but how am I supposed to know what the second month of middle school is going to be like.

I know that some things are going to change. My English teacher, Mrs. Bonnes, is going to have a baby, so she's not going to be at school at all next month.

I heard a rumor that we're getting a super old Zombie for a substitute teacher. I also heard that he retired from working at the local high school, so everything he teaches is really hard to work with. I just hope that the rumors are fake. I mean, they must be, right?

I have enough to think about without worrying if I'm going to have a freaky Zombie for my substitute teacher. I guess I just need to relax and look forward to what might happen next month. I know that with my crazy friends and my even crazier school, that something wild is bound to happen next month, and when it does, I'll be there to write all about it.

Book 5: My English Substitute Teacher

Day One: Last Summer

Dear Diary,

My name is Ugh, I'm a zombie, and I'm starting my second month of middle school, but I wouldn't be here if it hadn't been for all of the hard work that I put into my elementary school's summer school program, and with some help from my big brother, Roarbert. I was kind of a slacker in elementary school, which most people wouldn't think was possible, but it is--believe me.

During the school year, I had a bad habit of never showing up to class. Well, I showed up sometimes, just not enough to pass three of my classes. I got off lucky with that, too. If I had failed even one more class then I would have been held back for a whole school year. Since I failed three classes, I had to go to three months of summer school, which took up the whole summer.

In my first month of summer school, I took a history class which was taught by a Skeleton. She was hundreds of years old and had fought in one of the famous Skeleton Wars. I hate to admit that I was pretty rude to her at first, but that's only because I didn't know how cool she really was. I was a bit of a teacher's pet by the end of the class. Oh, I also made a friend named Snow. She's a skeleton and she's pretty cool and really smart.

In my second month of summer school, I had to take a chemistry class that was taught by a witch. Well, I think she was half-witch half-human, but that's not really important. It was a pretty advanced class for an elementary school kid, and I didn't do so well in the class at first. I even needed to sign up for tutoring. One of my best friends, Grunt, a zombie too, actually got really mad about it because I got a lot smarter while I was in tutoring and he wasn't. We had a few arguments, but we're still friends now.

My last class was a gym class. I know it was pretty lame that I even had to take a gym class. Who fails gym? Well, I didn't fail because I was lazy or anything. I just never showed up. I had to show up every day in the summer if I wanted to get into middle school. Believe me, there were a lot of days that I wanted to skip class. Luckily, I made some friends named Tibby, a skeleton and Will, a zombie as well. Hanging out with the two of them really made class worth it. Oh! The fencing stuff we did was awesome! It's probably my favorite sport, and I didn't even like one sport before the gym class.

Anyway, that about sums up my summer. I'm going to write a little bit about my first month of middle school tomorrow, but right now I need to do some other stuff.

Day Two: The First Month of Middle School

Dear Diary,

Middle school is a lot more intense than I ever imagined it would be. Well, maybe intense isn't exactly the right word. I would have to combine a bunch of words if I wanted to be able to find the right word. I would combine these words: cool, crazy, awesome, fun, hard, dramatic, and intense. It would be a really long word, to say the least.

Luckily, all of my friends who I went to summer school with passed it and got to come to middle school with me. School would not be nearly as fun if I didn't get to spend all of this time with my friends. I did a lot of fun stuff with them. Will, Grunt, and I had a lot of old-fashioned boy fun. We dared each other to do all sorts of fun stuff and we even had a big sleepover one day. The girls, Tibby and Snow, and I did some more relaxed stuff, like having lunch together and spending a whole day at the mall (which was actually more fun than I thought it would be).

My teachers also made things pretty interesting. The funniest teacher that I have is Mr. Nocab. He's a pigman and he's in charge of the home economics class. His class is really funny because a lot of the time he ends up eating the food that he's supposed to use to cook stuff, so he acts really weird about it. I don't know how to explain it, but it's really fun to be in his class. I even signed up for a cooking club that he teaches. I mean, Grunt and Will did dare me to join it, but I'm glad that I did. It's actually a lot of fun.

Anyway, I'm sure I'll have a lot to write about tomorrow, so I'm going to save my hand until then. I can't risk getting a hand cramp...it might just be the end of me...or maybe my laziness will be.

Day Three: A New Substitute

Dear Diary,

Today we got a new substitute teacher in my English class. Our old teacher is going to have a baby, so she's taking a vacation or something for a month. I heard rumors that we were getting a grumpy old Zombie as a replacement, but I didn't think the rumors were actually true. I still wasn't ready to believe them when I walked into my

English class today, but there he was.

"Mr. Marlowe" was written on the board. I could only guess that's who the new teacher was. He was a super old zombie. He had to be almost as old as Ms. Skele, my ancient history teacher from summer school. I wondered if they knew each other.

Mr. Marlowe waited for the class to quiet down before he began to speak. His voice sounded very deep and dry like he hadn't talked in a long time. "I am your substitute, Mr. Marlowe. I intend to teach you some more advanced work than your previous teacher taught you. You will be reading excerpts from great works of English literature. However, you will not be reading any of my work, as the school thinks that I would teach it in a biased way. Since we only have a month together, I will be focusing on famous authors like Shakespeare and his contemporaries." I couldn't understand half of what this guy was talking about, but it already sounded super complicated and really boring. I'm even surprised that I was able to write down everything he said without falling asleep.

I have a feeling that this is going to be a rough class, so I better pay attention. I'll write more tomorrow if this guy doesn't make us write a whole boring book before then.

Day Four: English Class

Dear Diary,

This English class is just about as bad as I thought it would be. On top of already knowing that the teacher was older than dirt, his teaching voice is the most boring thing that I've ever heard. It's basically like...I can't even think of what it's like. It's like the most boring speech that anyone has ever given, but times ten! I think paint drying sounded more interesting than this. It took all of the energy I had to just stay awake.

I tried to keep myself busy by taking notes, but even that was hard to do! A lot of the stuff that Mr. Marlowe was talking about sounded really complicated. It was like we were in a history and an English class at the same time. We had to write down all of these names and dates and the names of the people who these writers went on dates with! Well, not really, about that last part, but we were taking a lot of complicated notes.

Mr. Marlowe wanted to teach us all about Shakespeare. I don't know why, though. I mean, usually schools don't teach that kind of stuff until the first year of high school, and my class is only in the first year of middle school. I don't know what Mr. Marlowe was thinking, and I'm not really sure if he even knew what he was talking about. Whenever he talked about Shakespeare he seemed really angry.

He was saying how Shakespeare was overrated and how there were a bunch of other great writers around his time that should have gotten more notice back in the day and even now. He even said something about how Shakespeare was a jerk. It didn't sound very professional to me. It's like 'Calm down Mr. Marlowe, you're acting like he stole your fame, not some other dead dudes.' I didn't say that out loud, but I wanted to.

The other kids in the class didn't seem to like him either. Half of them were asleep by the time that class was over. I feel like this is going to be a long month...

Day Five: The Weekend

Dear Diary,

It's finally the weekend, which means that I have time to hang out with my friends outside of a boring old classroom. All of my friends were able to make it to the park where I wanted to meet them, except for Tibby. I asked Snow where she was, and she said that she was hanging out with Cranium. It took me a little while to remember who he was because I only met him once at a party that I threw. I didn't realize how close Tibby and he were. Maybe I'll invite him to the park next time so that Tibby will show up, too.

With Tibby gone, we had an even number of people at the park, so we decided to play a game together. Usually, I was always ready for fencing, but I didn't bring my swords to the park. Luckily, Will brought a ball with him, so we decided to play soccer. It was a little hard. One person from each team was the goalie while the other person on the team had to try to get the ball. It was a very personal match, to say the least.

Since Zombies are pretty slow, I decided to be the goalie for my team. Snow was on my team too. I knew that she was fast. Grunt was a little bummed that I didn't pick him, but I think he understood.

The game was on! The ball was

thrown into the middle of the park. I stood in front of my net and watched as Snow quickly got the ball away from Will. She ran the ball all of the way to Grunt's net, kicked it in...and GOAL! This happened a few times. Snow was a start player. I hardly had to defend my net at all. One time, she kicked it into the net, but Grunt kicked it out before it actually counted as a point. He kicked the ball so hard that it came right at me. I was frozen in fear and excitement. The ball went right past me! It was actually a little impressive.

Anyway, I'm tired out from all of the fresh air I got today. I'll make sure to write more tomorrow, though.

Day Six: Chilling with my Bro

Dear Diary,

I realized today that I haven't written about Roarbert much yet. I'm not actually sure if I've written about him at all. If I haven't written about him, then that must mean that we haven't been hanging out enough. He didn't seem to be doing anything today, so I asked him if he wanted to do something with me. He was still really tired when I asked him this, so I backed off.

I knew one sure fire way to get Roarbert out of his room. I put a pizza in the oven. Sure enough, Roarbert was out of his room a few minutes later. I told him that I would only share my pizza if he hung out with me. In response, he put half of the pizza on a plate and turned on our video game system.

Video games were kind of our thing. Maybe it was just a thing that all brothers did together. I don't really know, and I'm not sure that I really care. We have a good time playing video games together, and that's all that matters.

I guess I had kind of a lazy day today, but I think I needed it. I'm really not looking forward to going to school tomorrow. I'm thinking about pretending to be sick tomorrow, but I know that I shouldn't. I don't want to get stuck in my old ways. I really don't want to go to summer school again.

Anyway, I'll write more tomorrow. I'm sure that I'll be busier then than I was today.

Day Seven: Cooking Club

Dear Diary,

Last month I joined a cooking club, and it's actually pretty fun. I don't even mind that it's taught by my home economics teacher, Mr. Nocab. He's a Pigman who acts pretty weird a lot of the time. I swear he eats half of the ingredients for whatever it is that we're making that day before we even start cooking! He's a lot cooler in the cooking club than when he's teaching the home economics class. I think it's just because the cooking club is for fun while the home ec class is for a grade. He just acts more chill, and so do the rest of the kids in the class.

It's a little weird, I guess, but I haven't actually made any new friends since I've been in the cooking club. None of my other friends joined the cooking club with me, either. A good half of my friends are Skeletons, and they don't need to eat, which is probably why they didn't join the club. Grunt and Will did just dare me to join the club because they thought it would be a big joke. Once I told them how great it actually was they were a little jealous that they didn't join. I think I might even have the best grade in my home ec class because of all of the cooking that I do in this club.

Today we learned how to make hamburgers. I felt a little awkward to hear the word 'ham' since Mr. Nocab was a pigman, but he let me know that hamburgers were made out of cows, which made me feel a lot better. There're no part-cow people in the world, as far as I know. My burger turned out a little burned, but a gallon of ketchup made it taste pretty good. I had fun today, but I don't think I'll be offering to make dinner at home anytime soon.

I had a good time today. I'll write more tomorrow.

Day Eight: Crime and Punishment

Dear Diary,

    Mr. Marlowe was really getting on my nerves early today, and now I think he's directly on top of my nerves. I just wish I could fight that guy. Is it wrong to want to fight a teacher? Probably, but I don't really care. He just thinks that he can do whatever he wants to, and all because of a few kids messing around. I mean, he really shouldn't have been a substitute teacher if he didn't want kids to act like jerks to him. It's just what kids do. Besides, he's super old. He really should be used to it by now.

I guess I may have ticked him off, but not enough to earn the punishment that he gave us, not even close. Just to write it quickly...I may have hidden his Shakespeare book. I also may have called him Miss Marlowe all day. I also may have also gotten everyone else in my class to call him Miss Marlowe, too. For some reason, everyone calling him by the wrong name really ticked him off.

Anyway, that's when things got dumb. Mr. Marlowe got really ticked off at everyone, so he said, "Everyone must write a three-page essay about proper grammar, pronouns, and everything else that is related to calling someone by their proper name. It'll be due in two days." After he gave the surprise assignment he also gave us homework! I mean, who does that?!

Anyway, the whole thing made me really crabby, so I'll write some more tomorrow once I've cooled down a bit. Old Miss Marlowe really can get on a guy's nerves.

Day Nine: D is for Diploma

Dear Diary,

      The actual homework that Mr. Marlowe gave our class yesterday wasn't so bad. I made sure to put a lot of hard work into it to prove that I wasn't just some kid who screwed around in class all day. I needed to make it clear that I was a kid who screwed around in class all day and a kid who could get his work done. I did really well on my homework to prove that

I was smart enough to do the work, but also to prove that what I did on his fake homework, that essay that he assigned the class for calling him Miss Marlowe, was on purpose.

I purposely did a bad job on the essay just because I thought it was really dumb, which it is. I mean, the whole thing is totally unfair. Mr. Marlowe should really learn how to control his temper if he plans to keep on working with kids.

I had a smirk on my face when I handed in my no good essay. I even titled the paper "Miss Marlowe." If Mr. Marlowe has even a shred of a sense of humor, I'm sure he'll love it. Later, I saw him grading the papers, and I saw a big fat D on my paper. Needless to say, I don't think he liked it very much. Of course, a D is still a passing grade. It's like they say, "D is for Diploma!"

I told Roarbert all about this when I

got home because I figured that he would get a kick out of it. The weird thing is, he didn't get even a tiny kick out of it. It was weird. It seemed like exactly the sort of thing that he would do. He said that he was worried that I was going to start messing around in school again like I did in elementary school. I told him that he didn't have anything to worry about, but I'm not sure that he believes me. I'm not going to end up being a slacker again, even if Roarbert doesn't believe in me.

Day Ten: A Weird Favor

Dear Diary,

Today was really weird. Well, I guess that most of today was normal, but something that Tibby asked me was weird. I was sitting around at school, just hanging out with Grunt and Will, when Tibby came up to me and asked me if she could talk to me in private. It seemed really weird from the beginning, but I agreed to talk to her anyway.

Once we were alone she said. "I have a favor to ask of you..." She looked like she was waiting for a response, but I didn't really know what I was supposed to say, so I just nodded. "I want to go on a date this weekend--" I looked shocked. I didn't like Tibby in that way and I didn't want to hurt her feelings. Luckily, she finished her sentence before I had time to have a full-out freak-out. "I want to go with Cranium, but my mom won't let me go on a date unless I go on a double date. I was wondering if you could come with us and bring a date so that I can go."

This was a really weird favor to ask, but I felt a lot better knowing that she didn't have a crush on me. "I guess," I said. "I'm not really sure who I would bring, though. It's not like I have a girlfriend or anything."

Tibby seemed really excited to hear me agree to her weird request. "That's okay! You can bring whoever you want, even if it's just as friends. My mom just wants another pair of kids to come with us."

I did feel a lot better knowing that I didn't need to get a girlfriend by this weekend to make things work out for Tibby and Cranium. I knew that there was something going on between those two. Anyway, the bell rang for us to go to class, so I didn't get to talk to her anymore about it. I have all tomorrow to find someone to go on the date with me, so I guess I'll write about that tomorrow. Man, this sure was a weird day...

Day Eleven: The Perfect Date

Dear Diary,

At the beginning of the day I had no idea who I should go on this double date with, but by the end of the day I knew that I had the perfect person for the date picked out. With her, things would be super casual. I bet it won't even be weird to go on a date with her. It might even be fun.

I knew that I wanted to talk to a girl

to figure out which girl I should ask to go on the double date with me. It just seemed like girls knew more about this stuff than guys did. Besides, I'm sure that Grunt and Will would tease me if they knew that I was already going on double dates.

Since I had no one else to talk to about this stuff, I decided to sit with Snow at lunch so that I could talk to her about this. I told her all about what Tibby had asked me about yesterday. When I was done telling her all about it, I told her, "I don't really know who I should bring. I don't want things to be awkward. Tibby said that I could even bring someone as a friend. I thought about bringing Grunt along as a joke, but I don't think she would like that too much. Do you have any idea who I should take?"

What seemed like a total mystery to me seemed clear as day to Snow. She had a great idea right away. "Why don't you just take me? We can go as friends and it won't be weird at all. This way, you don't even need to worry about getting rejected if you were to actually ask someone. Unless, you've got a crush on someone?"

I didn't have a crush on anyone, and I told her that. I also told her that she had the best idea in the whole world. I officially asked her, "Snow, will you go on a double date with me--as friends?"

"Of course I will, Ugh. I love you--as friends." We had a big laugh about that.

Well, the double date is this weekend, so I guess I better get ready for it. I'll write all about it when it happens.

Day Twelve: The Double Date

Dear Diary,

    I decided to dress nicely for the double date today. My mom noticed that I was dressed better than I usually was. She asked me what I was up to, and I figured that I shouldn't lie to her. I told her all about the double date, but I made sure to tell her that Snow and I were only going as friends. Moms always take things too serious when it comes to dates. I knew she would tease me about having a crush if I didn't mention the "as friends" part, even though I don't actually have a crush on Snow, to begin with. Luckily, my mom gave me some money so I would pay for mine and Snow's half of the date. It was almost worth all of the questions she made me answer...almost.

My mom drove Snow and me to a restaurant that Tibby and Cranium were waiting at. It was a small family-owned place, so it wasn't very fancy. It was nice, though. As soon as Snow and I walked through the door Tibby ran us to us. She started whispering, "This is pretty last minute, but can you guys do me another favor?" I didn't know what she could want now. We were already at the date. Snow and I nodded, anyway. "Can you pretend that you're actually dating? I want to hold hands with Cranium today, but I don't think he'll do it if you guys are just acting like friends." It was a weird request, but I told her that I guess we could do it.

We were all at a booth, and Cranium and Tibby were already on one side. I sat with Snow, but across from Cranium. I didn't remember much about him, but I did remember that he seemed pretty cool. I figured we could get along well.

We ordered our food and made some small talk. It was a little awkward because I didn't really know what to do, but it was fun at the same time. I didn't notice it when it first happened, but eventually I looked down and noticed that Snow was holding my hand. My first instinct was to pull away, but Tibby wanted us to act like Snow and I were dating, so I just kept holding her hand. It was actually kind of nice.

By the end of the date, Tibby and Cranium were holding hands. They even hugged. I guess that means that Tibby's plan worked. This actually was a pretty good date. I had a really good day today. I'll write more tomorrow.

Day Thirteen: Girl Troubles

Dear Diary,

I woke up feeling a little weird today. At first, I thought that I was feeling weird because I might have eaten something funny at the restaurant yesterday, but I didn't feel like I was going to throw up or anything. I just felt...weird.

For some reason, I couldn't stop thinking about Snow all day. I haven't ever thought about Snow like a girlfriend but after that double date... I don't know. I mean, I know we were just going as friends, and I know that Snow only held my hand because Tibby told her too...or did she? What if Snow actually had a crush on me. I mean, I'm still probably too young to date, but the thought of Snow as more than a friend sounds pretty nice right about now.

I never really knew how to deal with these feelings since I don't get them all that often. I decided to try to talk to Roarbert about it. I don't think that he's ever had a girlfriend before, but he's a few years older than me so I'm sure that he's had a crush on someone by now.

I knocked on his door and he let me in. I told him all about the double date and my new feelings for Snow, and all he did was laugh at me! What kind of a jerk does that? I shouldn't have talked to him about this. The only thing he said between laughs was, "Ugh's got a crush..." and he said it in a sing-songy voice. It was annoying. That's the last time I'll talk to him about girls.

Anyway, I've got to go to school tomorrow, so at least I'll have something to take my mind off of this crush. I have the cooking club meeting tomorrow, so that'll be even better. I'll write about it tomorrow.

Day Fourteen: Nothing but Cooking

Dear Diary,

Going to the cooking club is just about the best distraction a guy can get when it comes to anything having to do with girls or anything else for that matter. I don't want to think about my new feelings for Snow. I'm even sure if my feelings mean anything. It will probably just pass and everything will be back to normal by next week. At least, I hope everything is back to normal by next week.

Cooking can be hard sometimes, and it takes all of my attention. I don't really have time to think about anything else while I'm cooking. That's actually one of my favorite parts about cooking. It's not super hard like math homework, but I do need to pay attention to what I'm doing if I don't want my food to burn.

Today the club was making stew. I always wondered how stew was made, but now I know. It's not actually as complicated as I thought it would be. I did have to peel a bunch of potatoes. It probably took me a hundred minutes to do it. Well, not that long, but it did stink. Making the rest of the stew was easy, though, and it turned out really well.

Mr. Nocab said he wanted to take the rest of my stew to test it and give me extra credit in my home ec class. I just think that he wanted to have a free dinner.

It didn't really matter to me, though. More extra credit for me! Less stew for me, though... Maybe I can convince Mom to make stew for dinner tonight. I'm going to ask her. I'll write more tomorrow.

Day Fifteen: Halloween in the Halls

Dear Diary,

I've been busy thinking about all of this business with Snow. I really don't want to think about it, though. I feel like if I think about it too much that it'll just mess up the great friendship that she and I have. I'd rather be her friend than risk not being her friend to be her boyfriend if that makes sense.

Luckily, I was distracted while at

school because it's almost Halloween. It's crazy how much monsters like Halloween. Even schools make special preparations for it. We got to skip two whole classes just to decorate our classrooms and the other halls in the building. It was really fun. I made sure to put up a whole bunch of colored-paper versions of Zombie's faces. I even made one that looks just like me.

When I got home my parents even wanted to put up decorations. I was pretty much decorating for the holiday all day. It was pretty fun. When I was done decorating at home my mom made everyone some poison apples. They're like caramel apples, but with poison. Since we're already part-dead the poison doesn't actually hurt us, it just adds some extra flavor.

Today was a great day. I hope tomorrow can be as simple and good as today was. Either way, I'll be sure to write all about it.

Day Sixteen: "Egging" on the Teacher

Dear Diary,

Class was a riot today, in every meaning of the word. It was hilarious. It was like a mob scene. It was beautiful. The best part of it was that I didn't even get into any trouble because Mr. Marlowe didn't even know that I did the prank. It was wonderful. It still is, actually.

So there Mr. Marlowe was, talking about something super boring, as usual. It was about the middle of class, which meant that about half the class was already asleep. I've actually done the math on this. The longer that class goes on, the more people that fall asleep. Anyway. I was starting to fall asleep too, but I knew that I would get in trouble if I did. I started to rummage through my backpack to see if I had anything to play with during class to stay awake. I would have even settled for a really cool-looking eraser at this point. That's how boring class was.

I kept looking in my backpack for something, and I found my lunchbox. Food sounded pretty good about now, so I opened it up, looking for a snack. That's when I found something even better than a snack. I found a weapon. My mom had packed me two raw eggs for lunch. Don't judge, they're good. It was perfect...too perfect.

When Mr. Marlowe wasn't looking, I took an egg out of my lunchbox and hid it in my hand. As soon as I was sure he wouldn't turn back around I threw the egg right at the back of his head. It splattered everywhere. I don't know what came over me that made me do it, but whatever it was, it was awesome!

When Mr. Marlowe turned around he was ticked off. "Who did this!" He yelled. No one answered. My classes weren't a bunch of snitches. Even if they were, everyone hated Mr. Marlowe. I was safe. No one told on me.

I didn't even get in trouble. All Mr. Marlowe said was, "I'll be watching you..." to the whole class. Sure, I was down an egg for lunch, but it was worth it. Man, today was great.

Day Seventeen: Everything but Studying

Dear Diary,

So, after screaming at the whole class just because of someone, maybe me, threw an egg at the back of his head yesterday, he may have mentioned something about a test tomorrow. I'm not sure if this was a quiz just because of the egg-citing egg incident, or if it was scheduled before that. Either way, I really didn't feel like studying. I had managed to stay awake during all of his classes, which is something that most of my class couldn't say they could do. This was good enough for me. I mean, just by being awake I had learned just as much as anyone else in my class would learn from studying, probably.

I decided to treat myself today, literally. After school, I stopped by the candy store and picked up a bunch of treats. I asked my friends if they wanted to hang out, but since we are all in the same grade they figured that they had to study. I was pretty close to bribing Grunt with candy to join me, but he said that he didn't want to end up in summer school again. He told me that I should study too if I didn't want to get myself in summer school, but I told him that I wouldn't let that happen.

I had to hang out by myself. I chilled out around the house and watched some horror movies, which I guess are just regular movies for zombies. My mom asked me if I had any homework, which I technically didn't, even if I should have been studying.

I ate a big dinner that night and I'm even going to go to bed early. Teachers always say to get a good night's sleep before a test, so at least I'm doing that. I'm going to ace this thing. I just know it.

Day Eighteen: The Test and another Favor

Dear Diary,

I took the test today. I took it so quickly that it probably didn't even look like I was taking the time to think about what the answers were, which is pretty much what happened. So, I knew some of the answers, and I filled those in right away. If I didn't know the answer I didn't waste my time by staying stuck on the

412

question. I mean, I was literally taking the test right then. I either knew the answer or I didn't. If I didn't know the answer I just guessed. It was all multiple choice and vocabulary, so I was done in like five minutes. I wouldn't be surprised if kids started calling me "Ugh the Speed Demon."

After class, Tibby came up to talk to me. At first, I thought she was going to compliment me on my speedy skills, but she only wanted to ask another favor from me. She told me that the double date went really well last time and that she wanted to go on another one this weekend. She wanted to know if I could take Snow again. I did something bad. I lied. I told her that I was busy this weekend. She said that was okay, and that she would ask someone else to go with her.

I felt a little bad about lying to Tibby, but the truth is that I don't really know how I feel about Snow yet. I'm still confused about everything since we had that date. The last thing I wanted to do was make things even more complicated between Snow and me, even if Snow didn't even know that anything was complicated. A weekend without a date will be much less complicated. Speaking of, it's Friday! The weekend starts now! I needed this, I really did. I'll write about whatever I do instead of a date tomorrow.

Day Nineteen: Some Friends...

Dear Diary,

Even though I told Tibby I was busy today, I really had nothing to do. I knew I couldn't invite her over or Snow, so I called Grunt. He was busy, too. Why must my friends have friends other than me? It's really annoying sometimes. Anyway, I called Will and he didn't have anything to do. He didn't really want to do anything today, so I offered to go to his place and play video games, and he seemed up for that.

His house was a lot like my house. There were plenty of snacks, the same video games, and he even had an annoying older brother. It was like we were clones or something. I tried to do the thing where I pretend I'm looking in a mirror to try to get Will to do whatever I was doing, but it didn't seem to work. I guess we're not clones.

We played video games for most of the time. When I mentioned that Grunt was too busy to hang out things got weird. "Yeah, I know. He's going on that double date with Tibby and her boyfriend."

This didn't shock me at first. It was only natural for Tibby to ask Grunt since I turned her down. "Who is he taking?" I asked while munching on popcorn.

"Snow, I think." I almost choked on my popcorn when he said this. "Are you okay, man?" Will asked me.

"I'm fine," I lied while drinking some soda to stop choking. Will didn't bug me anymore about the Grunt thing, but for some reason, the idea of him with Snow still bugged me. I had a weird feeling in my chest. I've never had it before, but I think I was jealous. I knew for sure that I was a little mad, too. I mean, why would Grunt think it's okay for him to take Snow on a date? Probably because I didn't tell him about my feelings for her. It's not his fault, right? I don't know. I need to calm down. I'm going to write more tomorrow, and I'm going to try not to think about this Grunt and Snow thing anymore today.

Day Twenty: Disguising my Appearance and Feelings

Dear Diary,

Roarbert didn't have any friends to hang out with today, so he invited me to come along to the store with him. He wanted to buy a costume for Halloween. Apparently, the middle and high school throw Halloween parties every year since everyone was too old to trick-or-treat. No one had told me this until now, so I didn't even think about buying a costume until now.

When we got to the store, I noticed that there were about a million options to choose from. Roarbert already knew what he wanted to be: a billionaire. He bought a white suit and top hat. He even got a fake gold watch and cane to go with the outfit. That guy really tries too hard when it comes to things that don't matter.

I thought about what would be cool, but then I started to think about what Snow might like. I mean, it was a school party, so she would be there. Usually, school parties had dancing too...so...

Eventually, I was able to find something cool and something that Snow might like. I found a fake suit of armor, like what knights used to wear. I also bought a can of paint so that I could make my wooden sword that I already had at home look like it was made out of metal.

Roarbert even thought that my costume was cool, so it must have been true!

Oh, I forgot to mention this, but I didn't talk to Roarbert about Snow at all while we were out. He laughed at me the last time I brought it up, and I bet he would only do the same thing. My feelings for Snow were basically the same, but now I was mad at Grunt for taking her on the double date. I really didn't like the feeling of jealousy, and I really didn't want to talk to Roarbert about it.

I'll write more tomorrow.

Day Twenty-One: Burning up Inside and in the Oven

Dear Diary,

I've been really crabby all day, and I can't really explain why. I'm still really mad at Grunt for taking Snow on that double date, but I can't really explain that, either. I've decided not to talk to him about it because I don't even know what I would say to him. I feel like it's best not to talk to him right now. It wouldn't be fair of me to take my anger out on him, especially since he probably doesn't even know that I'm mad at him in the first place.

I was so glad when it was finally time for my cooking club meeting. I needed to do something to blow off some steam. Today we would be making bread. This was great! Kneading bread was an important step in the bread-making process, and no one thought I was weird for punching the dough to knead it. Mr. Nocab thought my technique was great.

When the bread was ready for it, I threw it in the oven. Now all there was left to do was wait. Waiting was okay at first, but eventually, I started thinking about Grunt and Snow again. The thoughts really annoyed me. What especially annoyed me was just the fact that it was annoying me so much. I wish I didn't feel this way.

I was only brought out of my thoughts by the smell of something burning. "MY BREAD!" I yelled. I rushed to the oven then took out the bread. It was smoking and black. It was ruined. Mr. Nocab tried to assure me that I would do better next time. I knew I would, too. I just needed to get my thoughts and feelings under control. That's my new goal, starting now.

Day Twenty-Two: Ya Gotta do what ya Gotta do

Dear Diary,

As if my week could get any worse?! At least, that's what I was thinking this morning. I was already in a bad mood this morning. It kind of just carried over from yesterday, which is super annoying. So, I started off having a bad day. I thought that nothing could make my day worse, but that's because I forgot about Mr. Marlowe.

He handed back the tests that the class had to take the other day. As soon as I saw my grade my day got way worse. I had totally tanked the whole thing. There was a huge F written on my paper. Some slackers would say that the F stands for 'fantastic' but I knew that it stood for 'failure'. I was willing to let this thing slide and continue on with my terrible day, but Mr. Marlowe seemed to have other plans for me.

After class, he stopped me. He said that he needed to talk to me about some extra credit options. I told him that I didn't need extra credit, but he said that if I didn't get the extra credit I would probably fail the class and need to go to summer school again. I stopped and listened to what he had to say after that. "There is only one thing that you can do for extra credit. You'll need to sign up for the school's play. We're doing *Romeo and Juliet*. It wasn't my choice for a play, but it's what you've got to do."

I wanted to argue and complain, but I just didn't have the energy to do it. "Okay," I said. I knew I sounded defeated. "What do I do?" I asked.

"Show up to the auditorium tomorrow. You can pick out a part then and we can start rehearsal." I left the classroom. I didn't want to talk to Mr. Marlowe anymore. I didn't really want to talk to anyone. I'll write more tomorrow if I don't die from boredom in the auditorium first.

Day Twenty-Three: Taking the Easy Way Out

Dear Diary,

I showed up at the auditorium after school today. It smelled like damp wood and sad actors. I threw my backpack into a chair, sat down, and waited for Mr. Marlowe to tell me what to do. Moments later, he threw a script book at me and told me to think of who I wanted to be. I didn't really know much about the play since usually it wasn't read until High School, so I just asked who was already doing what.

I looked around the room and saw mostly high schooler's doing stuff. I tried to figure out who was the best actor or actress in the room. It didn't take me long to figure out that the best one in the room was a girl who was playing Juliet. That's when a great idea came to me.

"Mr. Marlowe, do you need any understudies?" He said that they did. "Can I be Juliet's understudy?" She looked like a perfect actress. There was no way that they would actually need me to act. There was no way I would be better than her. It was the perfect plan.

"I guess you can be Juliet's understudy," Mr. Marlowe said. He must have thought it was weird, but he still let me do it. My plan was going perfectly. I would be getting a bunch of extra credit without even needing to act. I am a genius. My week is starting to look up. I'll write more tomorrow.

Day Twenty-Four: Nonsense

Dear Diary,

I just had to tell my friends about everything that happened with Mr. Marlowe and the play stuff yesterday. I wanted to tell everyone about what I managed to get away with...everyone except for Grunt. I still wasn't in the mood to talk to him. I still didn't really know what to say or how to act around him. I didn't want to say the wrong thing, so, for now; I'm still not planning on saying anything at all.

When Grunt went up to get seconds at lunch I huddled my friends together to tell them all about what happened yesterday. They were pretty disappointed with me for failing my English test. Tibby gave me a lecture about how I was just going to land myself in summer school again. It seemed like Snow was going to say something, but Will cut her off, which I was kind of happy for. I didn't want to hear Snow say anything negative about me. I was still confused about my feelings for her, so I didn't really want to talk to her either. Man, if I don't get my mind made up I'm going to lose a lot of friends.

Anyway, Will interrupted Snow by saying how impressed he was with the stunt I pulled during the play practice. "You're not even going to have to act!" He was laughing so hard he could hardly talk.

"You sure did outsmart old Mr. Marlowe."

"What if the actress playing Juliet gets sick or something? You'll have to act then," Tibby said.

"Not going to happen," I said confidently. The confidence was fake, though. I hadn't actually thought about that. She looked pretty healthy, but who knows what could happen between now and the night of the play.

Tibby's comment made me realize that I should actually study my lines. I'll do that now, and write more tomorrow.

Day Twenty-Five: Ambush

Dear Diary,

So there I was, just walking in the hallway, minding my own business, when all of a sudden some heavy force pushed against me into an empty classroom. When I finally recovered (mostly from shock and partly from a now-bruised arm) I looked up and noticed that the force that had pushed me into the room was really just Grunt. Man, that guy had gotten a lot stronger since middle school happened.

"Dude, what's your problem?" I asked him in a not-so-polite tone.

"I don't know, Bro, what's *your* problem? You've been ignoring me all week. What's up with that? If I did something, I'm sorry. I'd just like to know what I did to make you so mad at me."

Maybe the shove helped me to get back to my senses, like how that happens sometimes when people hit their heads really hard. I didn't realize how much I had been hurting my friend until now. I decided to come out with it. "I-- Why'd you have to take Snow on that double date?" It sounded really stupid when I said it out loud. Maybe I should have tried that earlier, then I would have known I was being dumb about nothing important.

"Is that what this is about?" Grunt asked. He knew I was being stupid, but I was happy when he didn't actually say that

I was being stupid. "I just took her because you were busy and I'm not really friends with any other girls. I don't have a crush on her or anything...do you have a crush on Snow?"

It was time to admit it to myself, and Grunt, I guess. "I think so. I mean, I took her on that double date as friends, but we had a really good time. I've been really confused about how I feel about her since then. I guess I got a little jealous when you took her on the date."

"It's okay. I probably would have felt the same way if you took a girl on a date that I liked."

"Wait, who do you like?" I asked.

"Don't worry about it," he replied quickly. He also quickly changed the subject. "So, you like Snow? She's pretty cool. You're a little young to be dating, I don't really know what Tibby and Cranium are thinking, but Snow's cool. You'd be good together."

It was nice to talk to Grunt like friends again. The two of us tend to argue more than friends probably should, but we always make up in the end. I'm glad that we're friends again. I wouldn't trade my friendship with Grunt for a relationship with any girl in all of Overworld.

Day Twenty-Six: The Play: Act One

Dear Diary,

So far, my plan is working perfectly. The play's first showing was today. There was just one super cool guy that didn't need to act at all today--this guy. The actress who plays Juliet is wonderful at what she does. I didn't have a chance, but I never wanted a chance in the first place. I mean, I went to the rehearsals, and that's all that mattered as far as my extra credit--I mean, Mr. Marlowe--cared.

I even got two free tickets to the show. I thought about asking Snow to come with me for a real date, but I decided against it for a bunch of different reasons. It was partly because I wasn't sure if we would be better as friends or as boyfriend and girlfriend, but mostly because I didn't want to get rejected. I can't get rejected if I don't ask!

I decided to ask Grunt to come with me instead. I figured it would help us get on the path to being best friends again. Besides, some parts in this play were really funny, especially when you sat in the back row and had to make up what the actors were saying for yourself. It's hard to believe the number of fart jokes in *Romeo and Juliet* when Grunt is the one narrating it. It was great.

What's not super great is that I've got to show up to this thing tomorrow night. I'll write about it if anything different happens, but it'll probably just be boring since Grunt won't be here.

Day Twenty-Seven: The Play: Act Two

Dear Diary,

Oh man, my plan backfired and it backfired hard. The actress who played Juliet yesterday sprained her ankle after the show. She's on crutches and everything. Even though people say that the "show must go on," I was very much in favor of ending the show right then and there. Mr. Marlowe wasn't having my sass, though. He made me put on a dress. He shoved

me on stage, and said "ACTION!"

I never actually thought that I would need to act as Juliet in this thing. I was so embarrassed at first that I was having a hard time remembering my lines. Eventually, I got into the swing of things. I was really tempted to use a funny accent or something to make the play funny, but I knew that this play wasn't supposed to be funny. I actually tried to do my best.

It was weird to have to pretend to be in love with a dude. I mean, the guy who was playing Romeo was cool and all, but he's really not my type. He seemed a little weirded out by it too, but I think that just made him act even cooler about it. I mean, there was supposed to be this gross kissing scene, but he just pretended that we had made up a really cool secret handshake instead and then he gave me an awkward hug. Any awkward hug is better than an awkward kiss.

When the play was over I bowed and everyone cheered for me and the rest of the cast. It was actually a really good feeling. People threw flowers instead of rotten tomatoes in the stage, so I guess that meant that I did a pretty good job.

The play is over now, and some of the kids invited me to a cast party. Free pizza is calling my name! I'm going to write some more tomorrow.

Day Twenty-Eight: Halloween Treats

Dear Diary,

I'm really wiped out from my crazy play-going weekend. It was a lot of fun, but it was a lot of hard work, too. I even stayed up late last night to go to the party. Up until yesterday, I had no idea what my limits were on eating pizza, and now I know that I don't really have limits. My stomach is killing me today, though, so maybe I was just eating so fast yesterday that I didn't realize I had hit my limits... I don't know what happened, but either way, it didn't stop me from having pizza for lunch today.

I also got some great news earlier today in my English class. I had done a good enough job in the play to get a whole bunch of extra credit. I had no idea how much extra credit this thing was worth, and if I did know I probably would have taken it more seriously. Let's just say that I am now slightly below average, but still passing. It's a good feeling.

My cooking class was also really fun today. We got to learn how to make candy! It was super cool. We got to pick whatever we wanted to learn how to make. I really like gummy worms, so Mr. Nocab taught me how to make them look like real worms. If I had any human friends, I'm sure it would freak them out.

Since I was so full of pizza, I shared

my gummy worms with the rest of the class. Some of the kids gave me some of their candy too. By the end of the class, I had eaten chocolate in the shape of a beetle, sugary candy that looked like rocks, and black licorice (the scariest kind of licorice). This really got me in the mood for Halloween, this is actually tomorrow! I'll write all about it later.

Day Twenty-Nine: Halloween Party!

Dear Diary,

There was no school today, but there was a huge Halloween party at the school at night. It was really fun. I'm actually surprised that the school could come up with something so cool. Middle school really is a lot cooler than elementary school ever was.

I put on my suit of armor that I got while shopping with Roarbert and he put on his billionaire costume. We went to the school together, but we really didn't hang out much. I got some punch while I waited for my friends to show up. Snow was the first one to show up. She wasn't dressed up as a princess (she was dressed up like a mummy) but she sure did look like a princess. I didn't know what to do. She came over to talk to me. I asked her if she wanted some punch, but as soon as I said it, I remembered that Skeletons don't drink punch, let alone anything else.

I looked around for the rest of my friends, but I didn't see anyone else there. A slow song came on the sound system. "Want to dance?" I wanted to ask her that, but Snow asked me first. I finished my punch and decided to join her on the dance floor. I was super nervous. I felt like I was shaking. I actually didn't know if I was shaking because I was nervous or excited, or maybe there was a draft somewhere.

We got to the middle of the dance floor. Snow put her hands on my shoulders and I put my hands around her waist. It felt weird, but kind of nice. We started to dance in circles to the music that was playing. When the song was finally over, Snow started laughing. I couldn't help but think that I had done something weird. "What's so funny?" I asked her. I really wanted to know.

"Nothing. Dancing with you was just really fun," she smiled at me.

The rest of my friends showed up after the first dance. All of us danced to the fast songs together and ate a bunch of snacks. Snow danced to a couple more slow songs with me. It was nice. I even let Grunt have a dance with her without getting all jealous and weird. It was good.

The Halloween party was great. I can't wait for next year's party!

Day Thirty: Next Month

Dear Diary,

This month was crazy, intense, and a little crazy-intense, but it was also really fun. I have no idea what's going to happen next month, though. Today was Mr. Marlowe's last day of subbing, so our normal English teacher will come back tomorrow. Mr. Marlowe was really weird, but being in that play made me appreciate him more, even if I still don't like his random quizzes.

I did hear that the school is getting a guest presenter to come to the school. I guess the school is going to get a new woodshop class next year, or at least they are planning on it. They're going to have this guest guy show up for one month, next month, on a trial basis. I think I'm going to sign up for the class. I mean, at the very least, it'll get me out of gym class for a month. I'll wait until I see the presentation before I make my final decision, though.

No matter what happens next month, I'm sure that it'll be great. I'll be sure to write all about it in my next diary!

Book 6: My Woodshop Teacher is an Enderman

Day One: Middle School

Dear Diary,

My name is Ugh. I'm a zombie and I'm going into my third month of middle school at an all-monster's school. It's been pretty great so far, but I had to put in a lot of hard work to get here. Last summer I had to spend all of my time in summer school. It was rough, I only got weekends off. It wasn't all bad, though.

I had some crazy and cool teachers

and I even made a few friends. One of the coolest teachers I had was an ancient Skeleton named Ms. Skele. She was so old that she was actually in some important wars that are in history books. It was also during that class that I met one of my best friends, Snow. My best friend Grunt was in that class, too. We skipped a lot of classes together in middle school, so we were stuck in most of our summer school classes together. Grunt and I got in some fights in my science class during summer school. He was upset that I was doing better than him in class, but that's only because the teacher, Miss Enchantment, was tutoring me. She was strict but pretty cool. My last class was a gym class. Snow and Grunt weren't in that class, but I did meet two new friends named Tibby and Will. At first I hated the class, but eventually, I found some sports that I liked, which made the class a lot more fun than I ever would have thought it would be.

Once I got into middle school I knew that all of the hard work that I put in during summer school was worth it. The craziness didn't stop just because the school year started, though. I have one funny teacher named Mr. Nocab. He's a Pigman who is in charge of the home ec class. He tends to eat a lot of the food supplies, but the class is still fun. What's even more fun is the cooking club that he's in charge of. I joined it because Grunt and Will dared me too, but it's actually fun. I got to it every Monday.

Last month I had a wild teacher. He was the oldest zombie I've ever met. He was probably as old as Ms. Skele. His name was Mr. Marlowe. He was subbing for our usual English teacher because she had a baby. He was so mad all of the time. It would have been because the class was mean to him, but I think it was something. He also had this weird thing against Shakespeare, which was weird. I thought all English teachers loved that guy, but no...Mr. Marlowe acted like Shakespeare stole his spotlight or something. It was weird. I was really good at making Mr.

Marlowe mad. I might have even fooled around so much in class and failed a lot of homework. Well, that's exactly what I did. He made me join a play to get extra credit. I thought it was being clever by choosing to be Juliet's understudy in Romeo and Juliet, but the actress who usually played Juliet got hurt or sick or something, so I had to take over. I did a great job and all, but it was still pretty ridiculous.

Oh, I also may have a crush on Snow now. I'm still trying to figure out how I feel and if I should even do anything about my feelings. That about catches things up, though. I'll write more tomorrow.

Day Two: Normal Again

Dear Diary,

Whoever would have thought that a school filled only with monsters could be so boring? My old English teacher has only been back for a couple of days and I'm already starting to miss old Mr. Marlowe. At least I could get a rise out of that guy. Mrs. Pigtunia was a mom now. Nothing could faze her. It was pretty boring.

I almost wish that things could be

crazy again. Knowing this school, things are bound to get crazy pretty soon. I heard a rumor and saw some posters to confirm it, that the school is going to have a guest presenter on Monday. It's Friday now, so I don't need to wait for long. I guess the presenter is going to try to get kids interested in a woodshop class. The school has never had a woodshop class, so there is going to be a two-week trial class to see if it could work out. I might join, but I'm going to wait until the presentation to make up my mind. I've never really built anything before, so it might be fun to try.

Anyway, nothing super exciting happened at school today. All of my friends are getting together to hang out at the mall tomorrow. I'll write about that tomorrow. Anything we do then is bound to be more exciting than today was.

Day Three: At the Mall with my Friends

Dear Diary,

    All of my friends and I showed up to the mall today. It was great to see them outside of school. We could just do so much more stuff outside of school. The mall was our domain, and I had ten gold blocks burning a hole in my pocket. It was time to party.

    Grunt, Will, and I did some

shopping at the video game store while the girls and Cranium, he's Tibby's boyfriend, shopped for clothes. I felt a little bad for Cranium, but I've gone shopping with the girls before and it's not all that bad. I didn't really find anything good in the video game store, but Will found a sport's game. I've never really understood why people play sport's video games, but that doesn't mean I'm not going to play it with him if he asks me to.

Once we were done shopping all of us met up in the food court to have lunch. The food court was so cool. There was food from all over Overworld and even some stuff from the Nether. I didn't know what that stuff tasted like, though, so I just ended up getting a medium-rare hamburger. I sat down next to Grunt and Snow while we ate. I've been spending a lot of time with these two lately. Grunt and I are better friends than we've ever been, and I'm starting to wish that Snow and I were more than friends, not that I've told her that. I don't want to look silly in case she doesn't like-like me back.

After eating, we went to play in the arcade. This is what I had been saving up most of my money for. No one played air hockey as well as I did. I didn't get any tickets for winning, but I did get bragging rights, and that was good enough for me. I totally creamed Cranium in one round. He gave me some of his tickets because I won the bet we made. I did play some other games that gave out tickets. By the end, I had enough tickets to buy a pack of trading cards and some bubble gum.

Today was a really great day. Tomorrow I'm going to hang out with my brother, Roarbert. I hope that it can be just as good as today way.

Day Four: Lazy Day with Roarbert

Dear Diary,

After my great day at the mall yesterday I figured it was time to take some time to just chill with Roarbert. He's a pretty cool guy, but I don't really hang out with him all that often. I really should make a point to hang out with him more, but we pretty much do the same thing every time we hang out. It doesn't matter that we don't change things up. We pretty much always have a good time together.

Today we were pretty much doing

the usual. We slept in until our mom woke us up for lunch. She wasn't happy that we slept in so late, but I was pretty pleased about it. When Roarbert and I were done eating huge bowls of chocolate cereal we turned on our video game system and turned on our favorite game. We worked together to defeat hundreds of monsters in a virtual Nether. We were the heroes they always needed. It was pretty good.

Anyway, I didn't really do much today, but it was still a good day. Tomorrow is Monday, so I'll have more to write about. I bet that presentation will be cool tomorrow. I'll make sure to write all about it!

Day Five: The Woodshop Presentation

Dear Diary,

Man, that presentation was something else. I knew it would be something different to write about, but I didn't think it would be as crazy as it turned out to be. So, there I was, sitting in the bleachers. I wasn't really expecting anything amazing. I was just glad I got out of homeroom for this thing.

Suddenly, a strange creature entered

the auditorium. In an all-monster's school, "strange" meant something. It was unlike any monster I had ever seen, but I knew what it was right away. The presenter was an Enderman. I had only seen them in pictures before. He was a lot taller in real life. He strode into the room. Everyone was quiet. They were just as shocked as I was to see an Enderman in person.

He got to the center of the auditorium and introduced himself. His voice was really deep. He sounded like a supervillain. "My name is Mr. Violet. Today I'm going to talk to you about the trial woodshop class that I will be hosting for the next two weeks."

Mr. Violet went on to talk about some boring stuff that I only half paid attention to. It was actually kind of boring. He decided to build something right in front of us. He teleported out of the auditorium and came back with some wood blocks. I couldn't help but wonder where he got them from. Anyway, he took out not one, but TWO swords. He started swinging them around like crazy. Sawdust was flying everywhere. It looked like Mr. Violet was in a dust cloud. When he was done and the dust cleared away there was a perfect wooden statue of himself. It was kind of arrogant, but if I was that talented I would do the same thing.

I really think I might join the trial class, but Mr. Violet is kind of intimidating. I'm going to think about this. Either way, that presentation was way cooler than I expected it to be.

Oh, the cooking club was canceled this week. Mr. Nocab is at a teacher's learning conference or something for two weeks. He's promised to come back with some crazy new recipes to try out. I'll miss cooking class until then, so he better come back with something good. Anyway, I'll write more tomorrow.

Day Six: Should I Join?

Dear Diary,

I've been thinking a little bit about the woodshop presentation since it happened yesterday. It seems like it'll be a pretty cool class. I mean, I doubt Mr. Violet would actually teach the class how to do the cool thing that he did with the swords, but if he can do something that cool for a presentation then he probably knows how to do some cool stuff that he could actually teach a class.

One of the coolest parts about the woodshop class would be that I would get to skip gym class for two whole weeks because the two classes are scheduled for the same time. I mean, I get the urge to skip gym class literally every time that I have to go to gym class. I haven't done it...yet, but that doesn't mean that I haven't thought about it. It would be nice to have a real excuse to skip gym...

I've already talked to my friends a little bit about this. Tibby is totally disinterested in the woodshop class. It's probably because she's already in an art class when I'm in my gym class. I wouldn't switch art for woodshop either. Will doesn't seem to know what he wants to do about the club. He seems to think that it's cool, but he doesn't know if it's cool enough to join. Snow and Grunt want to join, but they haven't actually decided to if they're going to or not.

The only thing that's really holding me back is Mr. Violet. He kind of creeps me out. I've never seen an Enderman in real life before him. I've only ever heard scary stories about Endermen before. I mean, that was when I was a little kid, but the stories have stuck with me. Mr. Violet seems cool and all, but something about him makes me feel uneasy. I think it's his eyes...his glowing purple eyes...

Anyway, I'm going to keep thinking about whether or not I want to switch. I need to decide by Friday, so I've got to make up my mind quickly. I'll write more later.

Day Seven: Gym Class Stinks like Gym Socks

Dear Diary,

I had gym class today like I do every day. I thought about skipping, but I didn't, also like what I do every day. I guess my life must be pretty easy if my biggest problem is worrying about gym class, though. Today we would be playing one of my least favorite sports: volleyball.

Grunt and I were on opposite teams.

It was a recipe for trouble right from the start. Grunt and I are great pals and all, but that won't stop him from purposefully aiming the volleyball towards me if he can help it. The thing is, Grunt is really great at sports and I'm...well, not so good at sports, like at all. I guess I do play a mean game of baseball, but those skills won't help me here.

I stood in the back of my team, hoping that Grunt wouldn't see me. If he couldn't see me, then he couldn't aim for me. If only that actually worked. It was like the guy could sense where I was. As soon as he spiked the ball it started to fall in my direction. "I'll get it!" someone on my team yelled. My team knew that I stunk at this game by now. I dodged out of the person's way as they hit the ball...and as I accidentally hit the person next to me. It was pretty rough.

468

"Sorry," I muttered as I got back into place. I hardly had time to recover before the ball was flying in my direction again. I meant to hit it, but instead I just kind of froze up. The ball bounced off of the top of my head. It went into the air and another person hit it to the other side of the court. Stuff like this went on for the rest of the game. It stunk. Needless to say, my team lost and my head felt like it was going to fall off after all of the times that I was hit with a ball during the game. I ignored Grunt as he bragged about his victory. That guy really was a poor sport. Anyway, I'll write more tomorrow, if my headache is gone by then.

Day Eight: Making up my Mind

Dear Diary,

I don't know why I was having such a hard time making up my mind about the woodshop thing up until now. I mean, it should have been obvious. I mean, Mr. Violet still creeps me out a little bit, but we're all monsters here, so what does it matter? What really matters is that I dislike my gym class with a passion. I'm almost ready to run for school president just so that I can try to cancel all gym classes forever...or at least until I get out of middle school. I wonder if the school principal has that kind of power. Probably not. If they did, then someone would have already canceled gym class by now, especially considering that it's just the worst.

Today's gym class is what really helped me to make up my mind. Today we were playing dodgeball. If there's anything that I dislike more than volleyball it's dodgeball. Luckily, Grunt was on my team. My head definitely would have fallen off today if Grunt was on the opposite team. Grunt was a madman when it came to dodgeball. Let's just say that I would hate to be the guy who was on his bad side during a dodgeball game.

I'm not very good at dodgeball, to be honest. I'm okay at the throwing part of the game, but the dodging part. Today I even saw the ball coming towards me. Someone threw the ball. I saw it coming straight at me, but I was too frozen with fear to move. Seconds later, the ball smashed against my face. That's pretty much what made up my mind.

Tomorrow I'm going to sign up for the woodshop class. I heard rumors that it can be dangerous, but I doubt it's as dangerous and silly as a gym class. Who cares if Mr. Violet is weird? I just want to get out of this smelly class. I'll write more tomorrow after I sign up for the woodshop class and get out of this death trap that some people like to call "gym".

Day Nine: Signing Up

Dear Diary,

Today I basically kissed my gym class goodbye, at least for the next couple weeks. Even a day-long break would have been good enough for me. I went into the principal's office to sign up for the woodshop class. Snow and Grunt came with me because they wanted to sign up, too. Will decided not to join the class. He got over the fact that Mr. Violet is weird, but that freak of a kid actually likes gym class. I don't know what's up with him.

Anyway, it's Friday today so I need to wait until Monday to actually start the class. It'll be a little annoying to wait, and I still need to go to gym class later today, but it'll all be worth it. I just know it. Besides, there's no way a woodshop class with a guy as weird as Mr. Violet teaching it can be boring.

Tomorrow I'm going to go on a double date with Tibby and Cranium. I've asked Snow to come with me and she said yes. I don't know if she knows that I like her more than a friend, but I'm thinking about telling her. I haven't made up my mind on that. It's a lot more complicated than choosing whether to go to gym or woodshop. I'll write all about the date tomorrow, whether I tell Snow about my feelings for her or not.

Day Ten: The Double Date

Dear Diary,

I put on my best T-shirt for my double date. I wanted Snow to know that I was a classy guy, or at least, that I could be a classy guy if I wanted to be one. I even picked her some flowers. I have been thinking about telling Snow my true feelings for her, but I'm still really nervous about it. I don't want this to mess up our friendship if she doesn't like me back. I mean, I think she might like me back, but I don't actually have any proof that she likes me.

My mom drove me to the bowling alley where my friends were meeting me for the double date. I'm not very good at bowling, but no one is actually really good at bowling. It's pretty much the only sport that I know and that people don't really care if they win or not. On the other hand, Tibby is pretty competitive. She might just end up creaming us all. At least she's buying the pizza for us. That'll make up for any bragging she does later.

I gave Snow the flowers, and she seemed to really like them. She actually got me some candy while she was waiting for me to show up. That's pretty much the same thing as getting someone flowers, right? Anyway, we all played a game of bowling and ate greasy pizza. I only got 64 points...which is not a very good score. Luckily, Cranium only got 33 points, which made me feel a lot better. Snow got 99 points, and as predicted, Tibby destroyed us all by getting 128 points. I don't even know how she did it.

So, I never actually got around to telling Snow that I have a crush on her, but I think she knows. She's smart. I'm sure she's figured it out by now. I should still tell her at some point, but I think I'll wait a little longer.

Tomorrow I'm hanging out with Grunt and Will. I'll write all about it tomorrow.

Day Eleven: Chilling with the Guys, Literally

Dear Diary,

I didn't hang out with Grunt or Will yesterday, so we all decided that today would be a great day to hang out. It's November now, so the weather is starting to get colder. I bet it'll start to snow any day now. Even though we couldn't make a snowman today, the guys and I decided that it would still be fun to do something chilly. We went to the store and bought some snow cones. I got the blue ones. I don't even know what flavor it's supposed to be. All I know is that it's my favorite.

After getting snow cones my friends and I went to Will's house. It was his chore to take down his swimming pool. Well, it was his chore a few months ago, but he had been lazy about it. He asked us to help, and also dared us to do something crazy.

When we got to his house he gave us a dare and an ultimatum. "I dare you to jump into the swimming pool," he said. "If you do, I'll make warm brownies." I wasn't really convinced until he changed the reward to, "Well, my mom will make brownies," which was definitely a good enough reward to get me to jump into the pool.

Grunt and I borrowed some extra pairs of Will's swim trunks. We stood on the edge of the pool. "THREE, TWO, ONE!" We all jumped in. The splash was so big that the water went out of the pool.

The walls fell down. Well, I guess that took care of Will's chore. We went back inside. I was shaking from how cold the water was, but the brownies that Will's mom made were definitely worth it. Today was a pretty chill day, literally. I have my first woodshop class tomorrow, though. I'll make sure to write all about it.

Day Twelve: Woodshop Class

Dear Diary,

Today marked the first day that I got to skip gym class, I mean, today was the first day of the new woodshop class. I walked into the class and saw that the stations were divided into groups of three. I sat next to Grunt and Snow. I was sure that we were going to make the best team here.

Mr. Violet was at the front of the

classroom. His name was written on the blackboard. He actually had really good handwriting. Anyway, he also had a list of things that we would be doing in the class. Today was just marked, "General Introductions to Woodshop". It sounded pretty boring, but I guess that even a woodshop class needs to cover the basics.

The introductions were so boring that I'm not even going to bother writing about them. What I'm really excited about is what else we're going to do in this class. Later in the week we're going to go into the forest and get our own wood. We're going to make picture frames and birdhouses. I've always wondered how birdhouses are made, and now I'm going to find out. This class doesn't seem so bad, and Mr. Violet actually seemed pretty cool. I think I'm going to like this class. I KNOW I'm going to like it more than my gym class.

Oh, the cooking club was still canceled this week. It should be back next week, which I'm definitely looking forward to. I never thought I would feel this way, but I'm actually starting to miss Mr. Nocab. I hope he brings back some new recipes with him when he comes back.

Well, tomorrow we're going out in the forest. I bet that'll be really fun. I'll write all about it tomorrow.

Day Thirteen: In the Forest

Dear Diary,

It's a little embarrassing how excited I am to go to the forest and chop my own wood. My mom hardly trusts me with anything sharper than a butter knife, but today I get to use a real ax! Sadly, Mr. Violet isn't letting any kids chop down the whole tree. He says that he's going to chop down the tree and then we can cut blocks out of it from there. It's not super exciting, but I bet it will still be fun.

To get to the forest, Mr. Violet took

us one by one. He held onto a kid's hand and then teleported into the forest. I was nervous when it was my turn. I grabbed onto his pitch black hand. It was really cold, like ice. I held my breath as we teleported, but I don't really know why. We were there in a second. I felt like I was going to puke when I got to the forest, but other than that it was awesome!

Once all of the kids were in the forest Mr. Violet set to chopping down trees. "TIMBER!" He yelled every few minutes. I felt like a lumberjack. Once the tree fell, kids in my class ran towards it and started chopping. It wasn't even until the third tree that I got a chance to get any wood. The third tree was the craziest, too.

Mr. Violet was chopping as usual, but then there was a big gust of wind. The tree started falling in the opposite direction that Mr. Violet thought it would. It almost fell right on top of a kid! Luckily, Mr. Violet teleported him out of the way just in time. Man, was it close.

After we were done collecting wood we teleported back to the school. This was probably the craziest class period I've ever had. After seeing Mr. Violet in action, I almost think that we're going to have a crazier class than this in the future. I guess I just need to wait to find out. I'll write about whatever we do in class tomorrow, well, tomorrow.

Day Fourteen: Safety Day

Dear Diary,

I take back what I wrote yesterday about things getting even crazier with Mr. Violet around. Today we had the most boring day ever. I mean, I still would have rather been here than in my gym class, but that doesn't mean that I had a good time.

Mr. Violet made all of us sit through some safety video before we could actually start making stuff. I thought it was pretty silly. I mean, yesterday we were out in the woods, literally using sharp axes to cut down trees, and we didn't need to watch a video to learn how to do that safely. What can we possibly do in this classroom that's going to be more dangerous than cutting down trees? I mean, sure, we need to use a woodcutter thing to cut the wood into the right shape, but that's as bad as it gets.

At least I had Grunt by my side during the video. He was making fun of it the whole time. It wasn't hard to make fun of either. It looked like the movie was older than my dad, and he's not the youngest zombie around. Grunt kept saying that he was going to break all of the rules in the safety video. I couldn't tell if he was joking or not when it came to some of the rules, so I just talked him out of every joke he made. It was a little weird, but it was definitely more entertaining than the actual movie.

Tomorrow we actually get to make something in class. I'll write all about that tomorrow. I'm sure it'll be more fun than learning that it's not a good idea to use wood glue to stick your hands together. I bet someone actually did that once or else it wouldn't have been in the video. It was probably Grunt's uncle or something. Anyway, I'll write more tomorrow!

Day Fifteen: Picture Frame Day

Dear Diary,

Today was...hard to explain. It started out alright, but then it got kind of hectic. To think, the huge change happened in the space of about an hour. Then again, knowing my class, and especially knowing my friends, it shouldn't have come as a surprise.

Today we were making picture frames in the woodshop class. This was a pretty easy to think. Any normal person wouldn't have had a problem. Then again, my great pal Grunt isn't just any normal person, but that's getting ahead of myself.

All of the kids had to use a big electric saw to cut their wood into straight pieces. Mr. Violet was helping everyone with this, so it wasn't a big deal. After my wood was cut I went back to my table and started rounding the edges near the corners. I wanted to make the frame look like it was made out of bones. I'm planning on giving it to Snow this weekend if I get the guts for it. I'm also going to paint flowers on it, or add some real flowers to it, but I'm going to wait until I get home to do that.

When Mr. Violet was busy helping some other kid in the class with their picture frame, Grunt decided to do something silly. He was too fast for me to stop. He thought his wood was too long, so he thought it would be a good idea to use the big scary electric saw all by himself.

Needless to say, a silly zombie + a big scary electric saw = a recipe for disaster.

I saw it coming before he did. Grunt put his hand too close to the saw. A second later, the wood was shorter, and he managed to get a cut on his hand. It wasn't chopped off or anything, but I do think that he's going to get a scar from this whole thing, either. Mr. Violet teleported over to him as soon as it happened, but he wasn't fast enough to stop it. He rushed Grunt to the nurse's office, but he unplugged the saw before he left. I really think that Mr. Violet overreacted a little bit. I mean, it was just a small cut. I have a bad feeling about this, though. When one adult overreacts, the rest of them do too...I'll write more tomorrow.

Day Sixteen: Gym Again

Dear Diary,

The woodshop class was canceled today because of Grunt's little accident yesterday. I don't think it's fair at all. As much as I like the guy, I really think that only Grunt should have been kicked out of class instead of having the whole class get canceled. I wasn't that mad at first, though. I figured I would get a free hour or something to catch up on some homework, but then the principal told the class that

493

we would be going back to whatever class we were in before we started woodshop. For me, that meant that I had to go back to gym class.

Today we were just playing basketball, so it wasn't actually that bad. I mean, it's not my favorite sport in the world, but I'm not terrible at it either. It wasn't so bad to be in gym class today, but that's beside the point. The point is that I'm supposed to be in my woodshop class and I'm not. Hopefully, the school figures out what to do by Monday. I would really hate to be back in gym class on a Monday.

Anyway, tomorrow is Saturday. I don't have any official plans, but I am thinking about talking to Roarbert tomorrow about something important. I just hope he gives some good advice. I could use it. I'll write more tomorrow.

Day Seventeen: Following Roarbert's Advice

Dear Diary,

Today I wanted to talk to Roarbert about something that has been on my mind for a while. I knocked on his door and asked if I could come in. He let me come into his room without making a fuss about it. When I was settled in his room I got the courage to tell him what was on my mind. "I want to ask Snow on a date, just the two of us, but I don't know how."

The last time that I tried to talk to

Roarbert about this sort of thing he started to laugh at me. This time, he also started to laugh at me. I don't know what his deal. I mean, what was so funny about me wanting to ask out a girl? I was about to leave his room when he finally stopped laughing. "You're making too big of a deal out of this," he said. He was trying to hold back laughs still. "She hangs out with you all of the time. She probably already likes you. Just call her up and ask her out. If that doesn't work you can come back here and I'll give you more advice."

I didn't really know what else to say to him, so I didn't say anything. I left his room and walked into the living room. I picked up the phone and dialed her number. Her mom picked up, so I asked if Snow was around. She gave the phone to Snow. I nervously asked her if she wanted to hang out, just the two of us, at a cafe for lunch tomorrow. She said that she wasn't busy and that she would meet me there.

I hung up the phone and took in a sigh of relief. I could see Roarbert standing in the doorway. He looked a little too smug. Sure, his advice worked, but after all of the laughing, I didn't really feel like I needed to thank him. I walked into my room and ignored him. It felt good, but now I feel nervous. I have a date to get ready for! I'll write all about it tomorrow.

Day Eighteen: The Date

Dear Diary,

I put on my cleanest button up shirt today. It didn't have any stains or anything. I couldn't find any pants without stains on them, but we would be sitting down for most of the date, so she wouldn't be focusing on my pants anyway. My mom drove me to the cafe early so I could get Snow and me a good seat. I picked a small booth. Snow could pick if she wanted to sit by me or across from me this way.

Snow looked pretty cute when she finally got to the cafe. She sat across from me and we ordered our food. I was really nervous the whole time, but I don't know why. I had hung out with Snow a lot before now. There was no reason that I should be nervous just because I was on a date. Snow didn't seem nervous, but then again, I couldn't remember if I had told her that I meant for this to be a date or not.

After lunch, but before dessert, I gave Snow the picture frame that I had made in class. She seemed to really like it. So far, so good. When the dessert finally arrived I started to talk about my feelings. "So, Snow, we've been hanging out for a while now. I really like hanging out with you," I was rambling a little. I hoped she didn't mind.

"I like hanging out with you, too," she said casually.

"I was thinking that we should hang out even more," I said. Snow nodded in agreement. It was time to come out with what I was really thinking. "I was wondering if you would be my girlfriend."

The whole cafe seemed to get quiet, even though I knew that only our table was quiet. "Uh..." Snow seemed to be thinking. I didn't expect her to think about it. I thought she would just have an answer for me. "Let me think about it?" She asked. I said she could. I didn't want to rush her.

So, after the date, I went home. I may or may not have a girlfriend right now. I guess I'll find out when Snow figures out what she wants to do. Until then, I wait. I'll write more tomorrow.

Day Nineteen: The Cooking Club

Dear Diary,

The woodshop class is still canceled, so I had to go to the gym again today. It was really lame, too lame to waste paper writing about. Luckily, something cool did happen today. Mr. Nocab came back from...wherever it is he was. That's not the point, though. Now that Mr. Nocab is back it means that the cooking club is back! I have been waiting for this day for weeks. It was worth the wait, too.

Mr. Nocab decided to teach us how to make something that every kid wants to learn how to make: PIZZA! It was great. First, we made the dough. Mr. Nocab wouldn't let us throw it in the air like they do in the movies. He did show us that he knew how to do it, though. It was pretty impressive.

Once the dough was all spread out (by hand, not by air) we got to make our sauce. Mr. Nocab had tomato sauce for everyone to use. We also had little spice containers. We could put whatever we wanted in our sauce. I saw a lot of kids using Italian seasoning to cheat, but I wanted to be creative. I put in...well, the Italian seasoning, but I also put in some garlic and parmesan cheese. I knew it would be good.

Up next, we got to put on our toppings. I put on a whole mountain of cheese. I was ready to have the cheesiest experience of my life. I also threw on some sausage, but then I covered that with more cheese. Once I was done, Mr. Nocab put it in the oven. When it was done, there was cheese melting all over the place. It was so cheesy that it was hard to cut. It was the most beautiful pizza I've ever seen.

Today was great! I hope tomorrow is good. If not, I have some leftover pizza that will make tomorrow great anyway. I'll write more then!

Day Twenty: This is Lame: A Memoir of Woodshop Class

Dear Diary,

The woodshop class is back, but now I'm worried that it won't be as fun anymore. The school took away the big scary saw, which I guess makes sense. I mean, Grunt was the only one who was silly enough to use it without permission, so I don't really know why the rest of us shouldn't be allowed to use it. This whole thing really is a great example of how one guy can ruin something for the rest of the class.

The principal didn't kick Grunt out of the class, though. I thought that was a little weird. I guess it'll be nice to still have him in class. The principal did add himself to the class. He's not going to be building stuff with us or anything like that. He's just going to supervise the class. I think he's going to be here until the class is over. The class only lasts for another week, so I really think that he's wasting his (and my) time.

I'm a little worried that woodshop isn't going to be any fun now that it's being supervised. Mr. Violet seemed really nervous all day today. Class wasn't even fun. It was just boring, and I'm pretty sure that it's all the principal's fault. I'll write more tomorrow, even if the class is boring again. I hope it gets better...

Day Twenty-One: Birdhouses

Dear Diary,

Today we were finally going to make birdhouses. I have been looking forward to this ever since Mr. Violet said we would be making them. I've always wondered how they are made, and now I finally get to find out. I would usually be super pumped to do something like this, but the principal is still sticking around, so I doubted that it would be very fun. Now that class is over and my birdhouse is built,

I can say for a fact that it would have been more fun if the principal hadn't been around.

The principal made Mr. Violet treat us all like babies. It was really annoying. It was also making Mr. Violet's job a lot harder, too. The principal made him precut the wood for everyone before class started. There is a decent amount of kids in my class, so it would have taken Mr. Violet hours to cut all of the wood. I don't know a whole lot about how much teachers get paid, but I do know that he's not getting paid enough to put up with this stuff.

The principal didn't even let us use nails to put our birdhouse together. He was really close to not letting us use wood glue either, but Mr. Violet was able to talk him into letting us use it. For the whole class, kids were just gluing pieces of wood together. It took forever. The wood was having a hard time sticking together so my house kept falling apart. I was a little worried that it would never get made. Mr. Violet helped me out with some stuff and got the wood to stick together.

At the end of class, I left the room. Everyone had left their birdhouses together to dry. We wouldn't have needed to do that if we could have just used nails. But whatever. The principal is really cramping my style and ruining the whole woodshop class for everyone else. The class is over in a couple of days. I just hope that things will get better before that. I'll write more tomorrow.

Day Twenty-Two: Painting

Dear Diary,

Today was a lot more fun than yesterday was, and I think it's all because of the principal not being there. I think he wasn't there because we didn't actually build anything. Today hardly had any potential of being dangerous. Well, every day could be dangerous with a guy like Grunt in the class, but that's beside the point. Today we just painted our birdhouses. I know that it sounds pretty boring, but it was actually a lot more fun than yesterday's class.

We were given back our birdhouses to paint. We were allowed to put whatever we wanted on them. Grunt painted a bunch of flames on his. He wanted it to be the coolest birdhouse in the class, but a lot of the other guys in the class were doing the same sort of thing. Snow painted leaves on hers so that it would look more realistic. I didn't really know if that was a good idea or not. I mean, it would blend into the real trees really well, but I couldn't help but wonder if a bird would even be able to find it. I decided to make my birdhouse look like a barn. I know that birds don't actually live in barns unless they're chickens or something, but I thought it would be neat to make my birdhouse look like an actual house.

Today was pretty chill. Everyone in the woodshop class seemed to be in a really good mood. It was really nice not to have the principal around today.

Tomorrow is the last day of class, so we aren't actually going to build anything new. We need to talk about what we learned, what we liked, and what we didn't like and all that stuff. After that, Mr. Violet said we could have some free time. I'm excited for tomorrow, but I'm a little sad to know that the class will be over, and not just because I'll need to go back to my gym class. I'll write more tomorrow.

Day Twenty-Three: The Last Day of Woodshop Class

Dear Diary,

Today is the last day of the woodshop class, and I'm a little sad to know that I won't show up to this classroom next week. I feel even worse knowing that I'll need to show up for gym class on Monday, but I've been trying not to think about that too much. I need to enjoy this class while it's still around.

The first thing that we had to do was tell Mr. Violet what we did and didn't like about the class, what we thought about him as a teacher, and how we'd rate the class on a scale from one to ten. We took turns, going one at a time. Most of the kids said the same sort of things, mostly all good things about the class. Grunt made a joke about the tiny accident he got in. I thought Mr. Violet was going to give him a detention right then, but he kept his cool. I told him that the worst part of the class was the principal being there, the best part was learning how to build new things. I thought he was a great teacher and I rated the class 8/10. He seemed pretty pleased with my answer.

When everyone was done telling Mr. Violet how they felt about the class, he teleported out of the room and then teleported back. His arms were full of snacks. There was hardly a way that this class could get any better. Mr. Violet showed us some videos online of some cool carvings he was able to do. This guy was practically an online celebrity. It was really cool to see all of the different things that one guy could do with a chunk of wood. I hope there is a woodshop class next year so that I can learn how to do that stuff.

The party was the perfect way to end the perfect class. Tomorrow is Saturday, so I'm sure that I'll find something fun to do. I'm actually planning on just chilling at home all weekend, but my friends always want to do something, so I'm sure that something fun will happen. Either way, I'll be sure to write all about it tomorrow.

Day Twenty-Four: Thinking...Too Much

Dear Diary,

I put up my birdhouse in a tree by my house. No birds have moved in yet, but it's only been a few hours. I'm sure that a small bird family will move in before long. I just need to make sure that Roarbert doesn't wreck it.

I really should have planned something for this weekend because my friends are really bad at planning stuff. I had pretty much nothing to do this weekend. I mean, I didn't even have any homework to do. I was super bored. Being super bored gave me a lot of time to think...too much time to think.

I started to get worried about what Snow was going to say. It had been almost a week and she still hasn't told me if she wants to be my girlfriend or not. Come to think of it, she hasn't really talked to me much at all in the last week. I can't help but wonder if she's going to quit talking to me altogether. That would stink. I'd much rather be her friend instead of not being anything to her. I'm probably just worrying too much, though.

I'm going to try to relax a little bit. This thinking too much thing is making my head hurt. I'm going to try to take a nap. I'll write more tomorrow if anything eventful happens.

Day Twenty-Five: Snow's Visit

Dear Diary,

Today something unexpected, but great, happened today! So, I was sitting around in my room, just reading some comics and stuff, when my mom came to knock on my bedroom door. "Ugh, your friend Snow is here." I tried to remember if I planned anything, or if Snow did, but nothing came to mind. This was a total surprise. I quickly changed into a clean T-shirt before leaving my room to meet

Snow.

When I left my room I got really nervous. I had no idea why Snow was here. I couldn't help but worry that she didn't want to be my friend anymore. That probably wasn't it, though. I mean, if I didn't want to be someone's friend I would just stop talking to them and ignore them all of the time. Of course, she hasn't talked to me all week...so...I really had no idea what was going to happen when I walked into the living room to meet her.

Snow was standing there, not really doing anything. It looked like she was holding something behind her back, but I had no idea what it was. I nervously walked up next to her. All I could think of to say was, "Hey." It was a little lame, but it got the conversation started.

"I've been thinking about what you said the last time that we hung out together," Snow started. I was still nervous about where this was going. "Well, and...Ugh, just read this note." She had been holding a crumpled piece of paper behind her back. She handed this to me now.

I really didn't want to open the note. I couldn't help but worry that there was something bad written inside of the letter. I slowly opened up the note and read what was inside. "I will be your girlfriend." It was so simple, but those five small words filled me with relief.

I hugged Snow as hard as I could. Thinking about it, I haven't actually hugged a girl before. It was nice. Today was better than I ever would have expected it to be. I know tomorrow won't be this great, but I'll be sure to write about it anyway.

Day Twenty-Six: Good News

Dear Diary,

Today Snow and I walked into the school together...and we were holding hands. We weren't afraid of anyone finding out that we were together. Besides, I guess it was pretty obvious that we had crushes on each other. One kid from the seventh-grade class even said that he thought Snow and I had been dating for a while. Basically, our dating didn't come as a shock to anyone.

Even though we were pretty obviously together now, we still wanted to tell our friends what was going on, just so that there wouldn't be any confusion as to what was going on. Oh, and I kind of wanted to brag a little too. That's beside the point, though.

When it was time to eat lunch, Snow and I walked up to the table together and sat down next to each other. This wasn't really unusual or anything, but what was new was that we decided to hold hands while we sat next together. This got Grunt's attention right away. "Ooooohhh," he cooed at us. He had been waiting for a moment like this to make fun of us. The joke was on him, though. I had a cool girlfriend and he didn't.

Snow and I told our friends that we were dating, and they all seemed really happy for us. It was nice. Tibby was especially excited because now we would be going on more double dates with her and Cranium. Grunt and Will made a few jokes, but once they got those out of their systems they seemed to be really happy for us. I really hope that Snow and I date for a long time. She's a really cool girl. Today was nice, too. I'll write more tomorrow.

Day Twenty-Seven: Official Evaluation

Dear Diary,

Today wasn't as cute as the last two days have been. It was actually a little tense. It's not because of Snow or anything like that. Three days into our relationship and things are still going really well. I'm actually thinking about what I should get her for our week-anniversary. I think getting her jewelry might be a bit much, but flowers or candy might be just right.

Anyway, today was tense because it was time to fill out an official evaluation for the woodshop class that I took. It was pretty much going to be the same thing as what we all told Mr. Violet during class on the last day, but this was a lot more formal. For one thing, it was on paper. We needed to use #2 pencils. Every kid knows that anything that requires #2 pencils had to be important.

I felt like I was being tested as I filled in my answers even though I knew it was really just a type of test for Mr. Violet. I really liked him as a teacher. He was a pretty cool guy. I gave him good scores. If everyone else scores him like I did then I'm sure that there will be a woodshop class again next year. I'm just a little worried that Grunt and other kids like him will give him low scores as a joke or that the principal won't let him come back just because of that one tiny accident that happens. I mean, Grunt's cut is already healed, so I hope that doesn't cause any problems.

Anyway, we get to find out tomorrow whether or not there will be a woodshop class. I really hope there will be. I'll write all about the results, good or bad, tomorrow.

Day Twenty-Eight: Results of the Evaluation

Dear Diary,

Today the school came together for another assembly. Instead of showing us everything that the woodshop class could be, it was to tell the whole school about whether or not there was even going to be a woodshop class next year. Oh, and there was some pep-rally stuff, but that's not really my scene so I'm not going to write about that part. All I really cared about was if I could join the class next year. I was practically on the edge of my seat by the time the principal was ready to announce what was going on.

"I have to admit that I was a little nervous about Mr. Violet coming in to teach the trial woodshop class," the principal started. It didn't seem like this was going anywhere good. "While there was a small accident during one of Mr. Violet's lessons, most of the classes seemed to go well. At least, the ones that I supervised went well." The principal was saying things that made it almost impossible to tell what his decision was going to be. "Even though I may have had my doubts, after the student evaluations got back there is no doubt as to what I should decide. Every class had its possibility of being dangerous, but not all classes are as loved as this one was." This was starting to sound good. "Because of all of the great feedback Mr. Violet got, there will be a woodshop class all year-round next year."

A lot of the kids that were in the class started to clap and I couldn't help but join in. This was some great news! This not only meant that I would get to be in woodshop next year with Mr. Violet, but it also meant that I wouldn't need to take a gym class next year! This day really did turn out a lot better than I thought it would. I'll be sure to write more tomorrow!

Day Twenty-Nine: Student-Parent-Teacher Conferences

Dear Diary,

About three months of school have gone by, and so now it's time for the student-parent-teacher conferences. Usually, it's just parent-teacher conferences, but the school invited the students to come along too. I usually would have skipped something like this if I was still in elementary school, but since I stopped being such a slacker since I got into middle school I figured that my teachers wouldn't really have anything bad to say about me.

First, my parents and I went to see Mr. Nocab. I knew that this guy wouldn't have anything bad to say about me. He loved how great I was in the cooking club and I was pretty good with everything else in the class. Luckily, he did tell my parents how great I was. There was nothing to worry about. He talked about me like I was a shining star compared to the rest of the kids in my class.

We talked to my English teacher next. She did read off some negative notes that Mr. Marlowe left behind. I'm pretty sure that I'm going to get grounded for it later. She also read off his good notes, too, like how I pretty much saved the play that the school put on. That'll take off some time from my grounding, I'm sure.

Mr. Violet left some notes behind, and so did my gym teacher. My normal gym teacher was sick, so my gym teacher from last summer, Mr. Inferno, stepped in to read off all of those notes. That guy was pretty hard to look at, on account that he's on fire all of the time, but he had some okay things to say about me. Apparently, he didn't know I was a slacker in my gym class still, which was great.

Miss Enchantment was around to say some good things about me. She went on and on about how I really learned a lot from the summer school class that she taught and how I did a really good job of carrying over what I learned in the summer to middle school. She really was proud of me. It was nice.

I even saw Ms. Skele walking around the school. She was just there to pick up a check or something, but she still waved at me. It was nice to see her again. It's good to know that she's still alive. Then again, if she's lived this long then she'll probably never die.

Well, I'm home now and I'm only grounded for a week, so the whole thing really wasn't that bad. It was nice to see all of my old and new teachers in one day. I'm not grounded from my diary, so I'll make sure to write a little bit more tomorrow.

Day Thirty: A Busy Life and a Full Diary

Dear Diary,

I think this will be my last diary entry for a long time. It was great to write during summer school and a little bit through middle school, but things are getting pretty busy at school and with my friends. Besides, I'm starting to run out of paper. It'll be great to have these diaries to look back on later. I really did like writing in them. I guess it was a great punishment idea from my mom after all.

I have a lot to look forward to for the rest of the school year. After all, I still have Christmas break to look forward to, and Valentine's Day should be nice now that I have a girlfriend. Soon it'll be the summer again and I'll be done with my first year of middle school. Hopefully, I can keep my grades up so that I don't need to go to summer school again.

Well, these last six months have been great, but it's time for me to put down my pen and hang out with my friends.

Later, Ugh.

Printed in Great Britain
by Amazon